AF306733

Defoe Abbott Marx Hardy Melville Machiavelli Montaigne Haggard Chesterton Cooper Emerson Joyce Austen Hugo Eliot Grimm
Stoker Carroll Christie Molière Byron Schiller
Wilde Maupassant Engels Smith Kafka Hall
Garnett Fitzgerald Einstein Hawthorne Willis
Goethe Henry Dostoyevsky Kipling Doyle
Cotton Nietzsche
Baum Leslie Dumas Flaubert Turgenev Balzac
Stockton Vatsyayana Crane
Burroughs Verne Vinci
Curtis Tocqueville Whitman Gogol Busch
Homer Widger Tolstoy
Darwin Thoreau Twain Scott Plato Harte
Potter Freud Zola Lawrence Dickens Burton Hesse
Kant Jowett Stevenson
Andersen Cervantes Voltaire
London Descartes Cooke
Poe Aristotle Wells Irving
Hale James Hastings
Bunner Shakespeare Chambers Alcott
Richter Chekhov Shaw Benedict
Doré Dante da Pushkin
Swift Wodehouse Newton

 tredition®

tredition was established in 2006 by Sandra Latusseck and Soenke Schulz. Based in Hamburg, Germany, tredition offers publishing solutions to authors and publishing houses, combined with world-wide distribution of printed and digital book content. tredition is uniquely positioned to enable authors and publishing houses to create books on their own terms and without conventional manu-facturing risks.

For more information please visit: www.tredition.com

TREDITION CLASSICS

This book is part of the TREDITION CLASSICS series. The creators of this series are united by passion for literature and driven by the intention of making all public domain books available in printed format again - worldwide. Most TREDITION CLASSICS titles have been out of print and off the bookstore shelves for decades. At tredi-tion we believe that a great book never goes out of style and that its value is eternal. Several mostly non-profit literature projects provide content to tredition. To support their good work, tredition donates a portion of the proceeds from each sold copy. As a reader of a TREDITION CLASSICS book, you support our mission to save many of the amazing works of world literature from oblivion. See all available books at www.tredition.com.

Project Gutenberg

The content for this book has been graciously provided by Project Gutenberg. Project Gutenberg is a non-profit organization founded by Michael Hart in 1971 at the University of Illinois. The mission of Project Gutenberg is simple: To encourage the creation and distribu-tion of eBooks. Project Gutenberg is the first and largest collection of public domain eBooks.

The Scornful Lady

Francis Beaumont

Imprint

This book is part of TREDITION CLASSICS

Author: Francis Beaumont
Cover design: Buchgut, Berlin – Germany

Publisher: tredition GmbH, Hamburg - Germany
ISBN: 978-3-8424-4431-7

www.tredition.com
www.tredition.de

THE SCORNFUL LADY,

A COMEDY.

Persons Represented in the Play.

Elder Loveless, *a Sutor to the Lady. Young* Loveless, *a Prodigal.* Savil, *Steward to Elder* Loveless. Lady *and*) Martha,)*Two Sisters.* Younglove, *or* Abigal, *a waiting Gentlewoman.* Welford, *a Sutor to the Lady. Sir* Roger, *Curate to the Lady.* (Captain) (Travailer) *Hangers on to Young* Loveless. (Poet) (Tabaco-man) *Wenches. Fidlers.* Morecraft, *an Usurer. A Rich Widow. Attendants.*

* * * * *

Actus primus. Scena prima.

* * * * *

Enter the two Lovelesses, Savil *the Steward, and a Page.*

Elder Love. Brother, is your last hope past to mollifie *Morecrafts* heart about your Morgage?

Young Love. Hopelesly past: I have presented the Usurer with a richer draught than ever *Cleopatra* swallowed; he hath suckt in ten thousand pounds worth of my Land, more than he paid for at a gulp, without Trumpets.

El. Lo. I have as hard a task to perform in this house.

Yo. Lo. Faith mine was to make an Usurer honest, or to lose my Land.

El. Lo. And mine is to perswade a passionate woman, or to leave the Land. Make the boat stay, I fear I shall begin my unfortunate journey this night, though the darkness of the night and the rough-ness of the waters might easily disswade an unwilling man.

Savil. Sir, your Fathers old friends hold it the sounder course for your body and estate to stay at home and marry, and propagate and govern in our Country, than to Travel and die without issue.

El. Lo. Savil, you shall gain the opinion of a better servant, in seeking to execute, not alter my will, howsoever my intents succeed.

Yo. Lo. Yonder's Mistres *Younglove,* Brother, the grave rubber of your Mistresses toes.

Enter Mistres Younglove *the waiting woman.*

El. Lo. Mistres *Younglove.*

Young. Master *Loveless,* truly we thought your sails had been hoist: my Mistres is perswaded you are Sea-sick ere this.

El. Lo. Loves she her ill taken up resolution so dearly? Didst thou move her from me?

Young. By this light that shines, there's no removing her, if she get a stiffe opinion by the end. I attempted her to day when they say a woman can deny nothing.

El. Lo. What critical minute was that?

Young. When her smock was over her ears: but she was no more pliant than if it hung about her heels.

El. Lo. I prethee deliver my service, and say, I desire to see the dear cause of my banishment; and then for *France.*

Young. I'le do't: hark hither, is that your Brother?

El. Lo. Yes, have you lost your memory?

Young. As I live he's a pretty fellow. [*Exit.*

Yo. Lo. O this is a sweet *Brache.*

El. Lo. Why she knows not you.

Yo. Lo. No, but she offered me once to know her: to this day she loves youth of Eighteen; she heard a tale how *Cupid* struck her in love with a great Lord in the Tilt-yard, but he never saw her; yet she in kindness would needs wear a Willow-garland at his Wedding. She lov'd all the Players in the last Queens time once over: she was struck when they acted Lovers, and forsook some when they plaid

Murthers. She has nine *Spur-royals*, and the servants say she hoards old gold; and she her self pronounces angerly, that the Farmers eldest son, or her Mistres Husbands Clerk shall be, that Marries her, shall make her a joynture of fourscore pounds a year; she tells tales of the serving-men.

El. Lo. Enough, I know her Brother. I shall intreat you only to salute my Mistres, and take leave, we'l part at the Stairs.

Enter Lady and waiting women.

Lady. Now Sir, this first part of your will is performed: what's the rest?

El. Lo. First, let me beg your notice for this Gentleman my Brother.

Lady. I shall take it as a favour done to me, though the Gentleman hath received but an untimely grace from you, yet my charitable disposition would have been ready to have done him freer courtesies as a stranger, than upon those cold commendations.

Yo. Lo. Lady, my salutations crave acquaintance and leave at once.

Lady. Sir I hope you are the master of your own occasions.

[*Exit Yo. Lo. and Savil.*

El. Lo. Would I were so. Mistris, for me to praise over again that worth, which all the world, and you your self can see.

Lady. It's a cold room this, Servant.

El. Lo. Mistris.

La. What think you if I have a Chimney for't, out here?

El. Lo. Mistris, another in my place, that were not tyed to believe all your actions just, would apprehend himself wrong'd: But I whose vertues are constancy and obedience.

La. Younglove, make a good fire above to warm me after my servants *Exordiums.*

El. Lo. I have heard and seen your affability to be such, that the servants you give wages to may speak.

La. 'Tis true, 'tis true; but they speak to th' purpose.

El. Lo. Mistris, your will leads my speeches from the purpose. But as a man —

La. A *Simile* servant? This room was built for honest meaners, that deliver themselves hastily and plainly, and are gone. Is this a time or place for *Exordiums*, and *Similes* and *Metaphors*? If you have ought to say, break into't: my answers shall very reasonably meet you.

El. Lo. Mistris I came to see you.

La. That's happily dispatcht, the next.

El. Lo. To take leave of you.

La. To be gone?

El. Lo. Yes.

La. You need not have despair'd of that, nor have us'd so many circumstances to win me to give you leave to perform my command; is there a third?

El. Lo. Yes, I had a third had you been apt to hear it.

La. I? Never apter. Fast (good servant) fast.

El. Lo. 'Twas to intreat you to hear reason.

La. Most willingly, have you brought one can speak it?

El. Lo. Lastly, it is to kindle in that barren heart love and forgiveness.

La. You would stay at home?

El. Lo. Yes Lady.

La. Why you may, and doubtlesly will, when you have debated that your commander is but your Mistris, a woman, a weak one, wildly overborn with passions: but the thing by her commanded, is to see *Dovers* dreadful cliffe, passing in a poor Water-house; the dangers of the merciless Channel 'twixt that and *Callis*, five long hours sail, with three poor weeks victuals.

El. Lo. You wrong me.

La. Then to land dumb, unable to enquire for an English hoast, to remove from City to City, by most chargeable Post-horse, like one that rode in quest of his Mother tongue.

El. Lo. You wrong me much.

La. And all these (almost invincible labours) performed for your Mistris, to be in danger to forsake her, and to put on new allegeance to some *French* Lady, who is content to change language with your laughter, and after your whole year spent in Tennis and broken speech, to stand to the hazard of being laught at, at your return, and have tales made on you by the Chamber-maids.

El. Lo. You wrong me much.

La. Louder yet.

El. Lo. You know your least word is of force to make me seek out dangers, move me not with toyes: but in this banishment, I must take leave to say, you are unjust: was one kiss forc't from you in publick by me so unpardonable? Why all the hours of day and night have seen us kiss.

La. 'Tis true, and so you told the company that heard me chide.

Elder Lov. Your own eyes were not dearer to you than I.

Lady. And so you told 'em.

Elder Lo. I did, yet no sign of disgrace need to have stain'd your cheek: you your self knew your pure and simple heart to be most unspotted, and free from the least baseness.

Lady. I did: But if a Maids heart doth but once think that she is suspected, her own face will write her guilty.

Elder Lo. But where lay this disgrace? The world that knew us, knew our resolutions well: And could it be hop'd that I should give away my freedom; and venture a perpetual bondage with one I never kist? or could I in strict wisdom take too much love upon me, from her that chose me for her Husband?

Lady. Believe me; if my Wedding-smock were on,
Were the Gloves bought and given, the Licence come,
Were the Rosemary-branches dipt, and all
The Hipochrist and Cakes eat and drunk off,
Were these two armes incompast with the hands
Of Bachelors to lead me to the Church,
Were my feet in the door, were I *John*, said,

If *John* should boast a favour done by me,
I would not wed that year: And you I hope,
When you have spent this year commodiously,
In atchieving Languages, will at your return
Acknowledge me more coy of parting with mine eyes,
Than such a friend: More talk I hold not now
If you dare go.

Elder Lo. I dare, you know: First let me kiss.

Lady. Farewel sweet Servant, your task perform'd, On a new ground as a beginning Sutor, I shall be apt to hear you.

Elder Lo. Farewel cruel Mistres. [*Exit* Lady.

Enter Young Loveless, and Savil.

Young Lo. Brother you'l hazard the losing your tide to *Gravesend*: you have a long half mile by Land to *Greenewich*?

Elder Lo. I go: but Brother, what yet unheard of course to live, doth your imagination flatter you with? Your ordinary means are devour'd.

Young Lo. Course? why Horse-coursing I think. Consume no time in this: I have no Estate to be mended by meditation: he that busies himself about my fortunes may properly be said to busie himself about nothing.

Elder Lo. Yet some course you must take, which for my satisfaction resolve and open; if you will shape none, I must inform you that that man but perswades himself he means to live, that imagines not the means.

Young Lo. Why live upon others, as others have lived upon me.

Elder Lo. I apprehend not that: you have fed others, and consequently dispos'd of 'em: and the same measure must you expect from your maintainers, which will be too heavy an alteration for you to bear.

Young Lo. Why I'le purse; if that raise me not, I'le bet at Bowling-alleyes, or man Whores; I would fain live by others: but I'le live whilst I am unhang'd, and after the thought's taken.

Elder Love. I see you are ty'd to no particular imploiment then?

Young Lo. Faith I may choose my course: they say nature brings forth none but she provides for them: I'le try her liberality.

Elder Lo. Well, to keep your feet out of base and dangerous paths, I have resolved you shall live as Master of my House. It shall be your care *Savil* to see him fed and cloathed, not according to his present Estate, but to his birth and former fortunes.

Young Lo. If it be refer'd to him, if I be not found in Carnation Jearsie-stockins, blew devils breeches, with the gards down, and my pocket i'th' sleeves, I'le n'er look you i'th' face again.

Sa. A comelier wear I wuss it is than those dangling slops.

Elder Lo. To keep you readie to do him all service peaceably, and him to command you reasonably, I leave these further directions in writing, which at your best leasure together open and read.

Enter Younglove *to them with a Jewell.*

Abig. Sir, my Mistress commends her love to you in this token, and these words; it is a Jewell (she sayes) which as a favour from her she would request you to wear till your years travel be performed: which once expired, she will hastily expect your happy return.

Elder Lo. Return my service with such thanks, as she may imagine the heart of a suddenly over-joyed man would willingly utter, and you I hope I shall with slender arguments perswade to wear this Diamond, that when my Mistris shall through my long absence, and the approach of new Suitors, offer to forget me; you may cast your eye down to your finger, and remember and speak of me: She will hear thee better than those allied by birth to her; as we see many men much swayed by the Grooms of their Chambers, not that they have a greater part of their love or opinion on them, than on others, but for that they know their secrets.

Abi. O' my credit I swear, I think 'twas made for me: Fear no other Suitors.

Elder Love. I shall not need to teach you how to discredit their beginning, you know how to take exception at their shirts at washing, or to make the maids swear they found plasters in their beds.

Abi. I know, I know, and do not you fear the Suitors.

Elder Lo. Farewell, be mindfull, and be happie; the night calls me.

[*Exeunt omnes praeter Younglove.*

Abi. The Gods of the Winds befriend you Sir; a constant and a liberal Lover thou art, more such God send us.

Enter Welford.

Wel. Let'em not stand still, we have rid.

Abi. A suitor I know by his riding hard, I'le not be seen.

Wel. A prettie Hall this, no Servant in't? I would look freshly.

Abi. You have delivered your errand to me then: there's no danger in a hansome young fellow: I'le shew my self.

Wel. Lady, may it please you to bestow upon a stranger the ordinary grace of salutation: Are you the Lady of this house?

Abi. Sir, I am worthily proud to be a Servant of hers.

Wel. Lady, I should be as proud to be a Servant of yours, did not my so late acquaintance make me despair.

Abi. Sir, it is not so hard to atchieve, but nature may bring it about.

Wel. For these comfortable words, I remain your glad Debtor. Is your Lady at home?

Abi. She is no stragler Sir.

Wel. May her occasions admit me to speak with her?

Abi. If you come in the way of a Suitor, No.

Wel. I know your affable vertue will be moved to perswade her, that a Gentleman benighted and strayed, offers to be bound to her for a nights lodging.

Abi. I will commend this message to her; but if you aim at her body, you will be deluded: other women of the household of good carriage and government; upon any of which if you can cast your affection, they will perhaps be found as faithfull and not so coy. [*Exit* Younglove.

12

Wel. What a skin full of lust is this? I thought I had come a wooing, and I am the courted partie. This is right Court fashion: Men, Women, and all woo, catch that catch may. If this soft hearted woman have infused any of her tenderness into her Lady, there is hope she will be plyant. But who's here?

Enter Sir Roger *the Curate.*

Roger. Gad save you Sir. My Lady lets you know she desires to be acquainted with your name, before she confer with you?

Wel. Sir, my name calls me *Welford.*

Roger. Sir, you are a Gentleman of a good name. I'le try his wit.

Wel. I will uphold it as good as any of my Ancestors had this two hundred years Sir.

Roger. I knew a worshipfull and a Religious Gentleman of your name in the Bishoprick of *Durham.* Call you him Cousen?

Wel. I am only allyed to his vertues Sir.

Roger. It is modestly said: I should carry the badge of your Christianity with me too.

Wel. What's that, a Cross? there's a tester.

Roger. I mean the name which your God-fathers and God-mothers gave you at the Font.

Wel. 'Tis *Harry*: but you cannot proceed orderly now in your Catechism: for you have told me who gave me that name. Shall I beg your name?

Roger. Roger.

Wel. What room fill you in this house?

Roger. More rooms than one.

Wel. The more the merrier: but may my boldness know, why your Lady hath sent you to decypher my name?

Roger. Her own words were these: To know whether you were a formerly denyed Suitor, disguised in this message: for I can assure you she delights not in *Thalame: Hymen* and she are at variance, I shall return with much hast. [*Exit* Roger.

Wel. And much speed Sir, I hope: certainly I am arrived amongst a Nation of new found fools, on a Land where no Navigator has yet planted wit; if I had foreseen it, I would have laded my breeches with bells, knives, copper, and glasses, to trade with women for their virginities: yet I fear, I should have betrayed my self to a needless charge then: here's the walking night-cap again.

Enter Roger.

Roger. Sir, my Ladies pleasure is to see you: who hath commanded me to acknowledge her sorrow, that you must take the pains to come up for so bad entertainment.

Wel. I shall obey your Lady that sent it, and acknowledge you that brought it to be your Arts Master.

Rog. I am but a Batchelor of Art, Sir; and I have the mending of all under this roof, from my Lady on her down-bed, to the maid in the Pease-straw.

Wel. A Cobler, Sir?

Roger. No Sir, I inculcate Divine Service within these Walls.

Wel. But the Inhabitants of this house do often imploy you on errands without any scruple of Conscience.

Rog. Yes, I do take the air many mornings on foot, three or four miles for eggs: but why move you that?

Wel. To know whether it might become your function to bid my man to neglect his horse a little to attend on me.

Roger. Most properly Sir.

Wel. I pray you doe so then: the whilst I will attend your Lady. You direct all this house in the true way?

Roger. I doe Sir.

Wel. And this door I hope conducts to your Lady?

Rog. Your understanding is ingenious. [*Ex. severally.*

Enter young Loveless *and* Savil, *with a writing.*

Sa. By your favour Sir, you shall pardon me?

Yo. Lo. I shall bear your favour Sir, cross me no more; I say they shall come in.

Savil. Sir, you forget who I am?

Yo. Lo. Sir, I do not; thou art my Brothers Steward, his cast off mill-money, his Kitchen Arithmetick.

Sa. Sir, I hope you will not make so little of me?

Yo. Lo. I make thee not so little as thou art: for indeed there goes no more to the making of a Steward, but a fair *Imprimis*, and then a reasonable *Item* infus'd into him, and the thing is done.

Sa. Nay then you stir my duty, and I must tell you?

Young Lo. What wouldst thou tell me, how Hopps grow, or hold some rotten discourse of Sheep, or when our Lady-day falls? Prethee farewel, and entertain my friends, be drunk and burn thy Table-books: and my dear spark of velvet, thou and I.

Sa. Good Sir remember?

Young Lo. I do remember thee a foolish fellow, one that did put his trust in Almanacks, and Horse-fairs, and rose by Hony and Pot-butter. Shall they come in yet?

Sa. Nay then I must unfold your Brothers pleasure, these be the lessons Sir, he left behind him.

Young Lo. Prethee expound the first.

Sa. I leave to maintain my house three hundred pounds a year; and my Brother to dispose of it.

Young Lo. Mark that my wicked Steward, and I dispose of it?

Sav. Whilest he bears himself like a Gentleman, and my credit falls not in him Mark that my good young Sir, mark that.

Young Lo. Nay, if it be no more I shall fulfil it, whilst my Legs will carry me I'le bear my self Gentleman-like, but when I am drunk, let them bear me that can. Forward dear Steward.

Sav. Next it is my will, that he be furnished (as my Brother) with Attendance, Apparel, and the obedience of my people.

Young Lo. Steward this is as plain as your old Minikin-breeches. Your wisdom will relent now, will it not? Be mollified or – you understand me Sir, proceed?

Sav. Next, that my Steward keep his place, and power, and bound my Brother's wildness with his care.

Young Lo. I'le hear no more of this *Apocrypha*, bind it by it self Steward.

Sav. This is your Brothers will, and as I take it, he makes no mention of such company as you would draw unto you. Captains of Gallyfoists, such as in a clear day have seen *Callis*, fellows that have no more of God, than their Oaths come to: they wear swords to reach fire at a Play, and get there the oyl'd end of a Pipe, for their Guerdon: then the remnant of your Regiment, are wealthy Tobacco-Marchants, that set up with one Ounce, and break for three: together with a Forlorn hope of Poets, and all these look like Carthusians, things without linnen: Are these fit company for my Masters Brother?

Young Lo. I will either convert thee (O thou Pagan Steward) or presently confound thee and thy reckonings, who's there? Call in the Gentlemen.

Sav. Good Sir.

Young Lo. Nay, you shall know both who I am, and where I am.

Sav. Are you my Masters Brother?

Young Lo. Are you the sage Master Steward, with a face like an old *Ephemerides*?

Enter his Comrades, Captain, Traveller, &c.

Sav. Then God help us all I say.

Young Lo. I, and 'tis well said my old peer of *France*: welcome Gentlemen, welcome Gentlemen; mine own dear Lads y'are richly welcome. Know this old *Harry* Groat.

Cap. Sir I will take your love.

Sav. Sir, you will take my Purse.

Cap. And study to continue it.

Sav. I do believe you.

Trav. Your honorable friend and Masters Brother, hath given you to us for a worthy fellow, and so we hugg you Sir.

Sav. Has given himself into the hands of Varlets, not to be carv'd out. Sir, are these the pieces?

Young Lo. They are the Morals of the Age, the vertues, men made of gold.

Sav. Of your gold you mean Sir.

Young Lo. This is a man of War, and cryes go on, and wears his colours.

Sav. In's nose.

Young Lo. In the fragrant field. This is a Traveller Sir, knows men and manners, and has plow'd up the Sea so far till both the Poles have knockt, has seen the Sun take Coach, and can distinguish the colour of his Horses, and their kinds, and had a *Flanders*-Mare leapt there.

Sav. 'Tis much.

Tra. I have seen more Sir.

Sav. 'Tis even enough o' Conscience; sit down, and rest you, you are at the end of the world already. Would you had as good a Living Sir, as this fellow could lie you out of, he has a notable gift in't.

Young Lo. This ministers the smoak, and this the Muses.

Sav. And you the Cloaths, and Meat, and Money, you have a goodly generation of 'em, pray let them multiply, your Brother's house is big enough, and to say truth, h'as too much Land, hang it durt.

Young Lo. Why now thou art a loving stinkard. Fire off thy Annotations and thy Rent-books, thou hast a weak brain *Savil*, and with the next long Bill thou wilt run mad. Gentlemen, you are once more welcome to three hundred pounds a year; we will be freely merry, shall we not?

Capt. Merry as mirth and wine, my lovely *Loveless*.

Poet. A serious look shall be a Jury to excommunicate any man from our company.

Tra. We will not talk wisely neither?

Young Lo. What think you Gentlemen by all this Revenue in Drink?

Capt. I am all for Drink.

Tra. I am dry till it be so.

Poet. He that will not cry Amen to this, let him live sober, seem wise, and dye o'th' *Coram.*

Young Lo. It shall be so, we'l have it all in Drink, let Meat and Lodging go, they are transitory, and shew men meerly mortal: then we'l have Wenches, every one his Wench, and every week a fresh one: we'l keep no powdered flesh: all these we have by warrant, under the title of things necessary. Here upon this place I ground it, The obedience of my people, and all necessaries: your opinions Gentlemen?

Capt. 'Tis plain and evident that he meant Wenches.

Sav. Good Sir let me expound it?

Capt. Here be as sound men, as your self Sir.

Poet. This do I hold to be the interpretation of it: In this word Necessary, is concluded all that be helps to Man; Woman was made the first, and therefore here the chiefest.

Young Lo. Believe me 'tis a learned one; and by these words, The obedience of my people, you Steward being one, are bound to fetch us Wenches.

Capt. He is, he is.

Young Lo. Steward, attend us for instructions.

Sav. But will you keep no house Sir?

Young Lo. Nothing but drink Sir, three hundred pounds in drink.

Sav. O miserable house, and miserable I that live to see it! Good Sir keep some meat.

Young Lo. Get us good Whores, and for your part, I'le board you in an Alehouse, you shall have Cheese and Onions.

Sav. What shall become of me, no Chimney smoaking? Well Prodigal, your Brother will come home.

[*Exit.*

Young Lo. Come Lads, I'le warrant you for Wenches, three hundred pounds in drink.

[*Exeunt omnes.*

Actus Secundus. Scena Prima.

_Enter Lady, *her Sister* Martha, Welford, Younglove, *and others.*

Lady. Sir, now you see your bad lodging, I must bid you good night.

Wel. Lady if there be any want, 'tis in want of you.

Lady. A little sleep will ease that complement. Once more good night.

Wel. Once more dear Lady, and then all sweet nights.

Lady. Dear Sir be short and sweet then.

Wel. Shall the morrow prove better to me, shall I hope my sute happier by this nights rest?

Lady. Is your sute so sickly that rest will help it? Pray ye let it rest then till I call for it. Sir as a stranger you have had all my welcome: but had I known your errand ere you came, your passage had been straiter. Sir, good night.

Welford. So fair, and cruel, dear unkind good night. [*Exit* Lady. Nay Sir, you shall stay with me, I'le press your zeal so far.

Roger. O Lord Sir.

Wel. Do you love *Tobacco*?

Rog. Surely I love it, but it loves not me; yet with your reverence I'le be bold.

Wel. Pray light it Sir. How do you like it?

Rog. I promise you it is notable stinging geer indeed. It is wet Sir, Lord how it brings down Rheum!

Wel. Handle it again Sir, you have a warm text of it.

Rog. Thanks ever promised for it. I promise you it is very powerful, and by a Trope, spiritual; for certainly it moves in sundry places.

Wel. I, it does so Sir, and me especially to ask Sir, why you wear a Night-cap.

Rog. Assuredly I will speak the truth unto you: you shall understand Sir, that my head is broken, and by whom; even by that visible beast the Butler.

Wel. The Butler? certainly he had all his drink about him when he did it. Strike one of your grave Cassock? The offence Sir?

Rog. Reproving him at Tra-trip Sir, for swearing; you have the total surely.

Wel. You told him when his rage was set a tilt, and so he crackt your Canons. I hope he has not hurt your gentle reading: But shall we see these Gentlewomen to night.

Rog. Have patience Sir until our fellow *Nicholas* be deceast, that is, asleep: for so the word is taken: to sleep to dye, to dye to sleep, a very figure Sir.

Wel. Cannot you cast another for the Gentlewomen?

Rog. Not till the man be in his bed, his grave: his grave, his bed: the very same again Sir. Our Comick Poet gives the reason sweetly; *Plenus rimarum est,* he is full of loope-holes, and will discover to our Patroness.

Wel. Your comment Sir has made me understand you.

Enter Martha *the* Ladies *Sister, and* Younglove, *to them with a Posset.*

Rog. Sir be addrest, the graces do salute you with the full bowl of plenty. Is our old enemy entomb'd?

Abig. He's safe.

Rog. And does he snore out supinely with the Poet?

Mar. No, he out-snores the Poet.

Wel. Gentlewoman, this courtesie shall bind a stranger to you, ever your servant.

Mar. Sir, my Sisters strictness makes not us forget you are a stranger and a Gentleman.

Abig. In sooth Sir, were I chang'd into my Lady, a Gentleman so well indued with parts, should not be lost.

Wel. I thank you Gentlewoman, and rest bound to you. See how this foul familiar chewes the Cud: From thee, and three and fifty good Love deliver me.

Mar. Will you sit down Sir, and take a spoon?

Wel. I take it kindly, Lady.

Mar. It is our best banquet Sir.

Rog. Shall we give thanks?

Wel. I have to the Gentlewomen already Sir.

Mar. Good Sir *Roger*, keep that breath to cool your part o'th' Posset, you may chance have a scalding zeal else; and you will needs be doing, pray tell your twenty to your self. Would you could like this Sir?

Wel. I would your Sister would like me as well Lady.

Mar. Sure Sir, she would not eat you: but banish that imagination; she's only wedded to her self, lyes with her self, and loves her self; and for another Husband than herself, he may knock at the gate, but ne're come in: be wise Sir, she's a Woman, and a trouble, and has her many faults, the least of which is, she cannot love you.

Abig. God pardon her, she'l do worse, would I were worthy his least grief, Mistris *Martha*.

Wel. Now I must over-hear her.

Mar. Faith would thou hadst them all with all my heart; I do not think they would make thee a day older.

Abig. Sir, will you put in deeper, 'tis the sweeter.

Mar. Well said old sayings.

Wel. She looks like one indeed. Gentlewoman you keep your word, your sweet self has made the bottom sweeter.

Abig. Sir, I begin a frolick, dare you change Sir?

Wel. My self for you, so please you. That smile has turn'd my stomach: this is right the old Embleme of the Moyle cropping of Thistles: Lord what a hunting head she carries, sure she has been ridden with a Martingale. Now love deliver me.

Rog. Do I dream, or do I wake? surely I know not: am I rub'd off? Is this the way of all my morning Prayers? Oh *Roger*, thou art but grass, and woman as a flower. Did I for this consume my quarters in Meditation, Vowes, and wooed her in *Heroical Epistles*? Did I expound the Owl, and undertook with labour and expence the recollection of those thousand Pieces, consum'd in Cellars, and Tab-acco-shops of that our honour'd *Englishman Ni. Br.*? Have I done this, and am I done thus too? I will end with the wise man, and say; He that holds a Woman, has an Eel by the tail.

Mar. Sir 'tis so late, and our entertainment (meaning our Posset) by this is grown so cold, that 'twere an unmannerly part longer to hold you from your rest: let what the house has be at your com-mand Sir.

Wel. Sweet rest be with you Lady; and to you what you desire too.

Abig. It should be some such good thing like your self then. [*Exeunt.*

Wel. Heaven keep me from that curse, and all my issue. Good night Antiquity.

Rog. Solamen Miseris socios habuisse Doloris: but I alone.

Wel. Learned Sir, will you bid my man come to me? and re-questing a greater measure of your learning, good night, good Mas-ter *Roger*.

Rog. Good Sir, peace be with you. [*Exit* Roger.

Wel. Adue dear *Domine.* Half a dozen such in a Kingdom would make a man forswear confession: for who that had but half his wits about him, would commit the Counsel of a serious sin to such a cruel Night-cap? Why how now shall we have an Antick? [*Enter Servant.* Whose head do you carry upon your shoulders, that you jole it so against the Post? Is't for your ease? Or have you seen the Celler? Where are my slippers Sir?

Ser. Here Sir.

Wel. Where Sir? have you got the pot Verdugo? have you seen the Horses Sir?

Ser. Yes Sir.

Wel. Have they any meat?

Ser. Faith Sir, they have a kind of wholesome Rushes, Hay I cannot call it.

Wel. And no Provender?

Ser. Sir, so I take it.

Wel. You are merry Sir, and why so?

Ser. Faith Sir, here are no Oats to be got, unless you'l have 'em in Porredge: the people are so mainly given to spoon-meat: yonder's a cast of Coach-mares of the Gentlewomans, the strangest Cattel.

Wel. Why?

Ser. Why, they are transparent Sir, you may see through them: and such a house!

Wel. Come Sir, the truth of your discovery.

Ser. Sir, they are in tribes like Jewes: the Kitchin and the Dayrie make one tribe, and have their faction and their fornication within themselves; the Buttery and the Landry are another, and there's no love lost; the chambers are intire, and what's done there, is somewhat higher than my knowledge: but this I am sure, between these copulations, a stranger is kept vertuous, that is, fasting. But of all this the drink Sir.

Wel. What of that Sir?

_Ser. _Faith Sir, I will handle it as the time and your patience will give me leave. This drink, or this cooling Julip, of which three spoonfuls kills the Calenture, a pint breeds the cold Palsie.

_Wel. _Sir, you bely the house.

_Ser. _I would I did Sir. But as I am a true man, if 'twere but one degree colder, nothing but an Asses hoof would hold it.

_Wel. _I am glad on't Sir, for if it had proved stronger, you had been tongue ti'd of these commendations. Light me the candle Sir, I'le hear no more. [*Exeunt.*

Enter young Loveless _and his _Comrades, *with wenches, and two Fidlers.*

_Yo. Lo. _Come my brave man of war, trace out thy darling,
And you my learned Council, sit and turn boyes,
Kiss till the Cow come home, kiss close, kiss close knaves.
My Modern Poet, thou shalt kiss in couplets.

Enter with Wine.

Strike up you merry varlets, and leave your peeping,
This is no pay for Fidlers.

Capt. O my dear boy, thy *Hercules,* thy Captain
Makes thee his *Hylas,* his delight, his solace.
Love thy brave man of war, and let thy bounty
Clap him in *Shamois*: Let there be deducted out of our main potation
Five Marks in hatchments to adorn this thigh,
Crampt with this rest of peace, and I will fight
Thy battels.

Yo. Lo. Thou shalt hav't boy, and fly in Feather, Lead on a March you Michers.

Enter Savill.

Savill. O my head, O my heart, what a noyse and change is here! would I had been cold i'th' mouth before this day, and ne're have liv'd to see this dissolution. He that lives within a mile of this place, had as good sleep in the perpetual noyse of an Iron Mill. There's a dead Sea of drink i'th' Seller, in which goodly vessels lye wrackt, and in the middle of this deluge appear the tops of flagons and black jacks, like Churches drown'd i'th' marshes.

Yo. Lo. What, art thou come? My sweet Sir *Amias* welcome to *Troy.* Come thou shalt kiss my *Helen,* and court her in a dance.

Sav. Good Sir consider?

Yo. Lo. Shall we consider Gentlemen? How say you?

Capt. Consider? that were a simple toy i'faith, consider? whose moral's that? The man that cryes consider is our foe: let my steel know him.

Young Lo. Stay thy dead doing hand, he must not die yet: prethee be calm my *Hector.*

Capt. Peasant slave, thou groom compos'd of grudgings, live and thank this Gentleman, thou hadst seen *Pluto* else. The next consider kills thee.

Trav. Let him drink down his word again in a gallon of Sack.

Poet. 'Tis but a snuffe, make it two gallons, and let him doe it kneeling in repentance.

Savil. Nay rather kill me, there's but a lay-man lost. Good Captain doe your office.

Young Lo. Thou shalt drink Steward, drink and dance my Steward. Strike him a horn-pipe squeakers, take thy striver, and pace her till she stew.

Savil. Sure Sir, I cannot dance with your Gentlewomen, they are too light for me, pray break my head, and let me goe.

Capt. He shall dance, he shall dance.

Young Lo. He shall dance, and drink, and be drunk and dance, and be drunk again, and shall see no meat in a year.

Poet. And three quarters?

Young Lo. And three quarters be it.

Capt. Who knocks there? let him in.

Enter Elder Loveless *disguised.*

Suvill. Some to deliver me I hope.

Elder Lo. Gentlemen, God save you all, my business is to one Master *Loveless*?

Capt. This is the Gentleman you mean; view him, and take his Inventorie, he's a right one.

Elder Lo. He promises no less Sir.

Young Lo. Sir, your business?

Elder Lo. Sir, I should let you know, yet I am loth, yet I am sworn to't, would some other tongue would speak it for me.

Young Lo. Out with it i' Gods name.

Elder Lo. All I desire Sir is, the patience and sufferance of a man, and good Sir be not mov'd more.

Young Lo. Then a pottle of sack will doe, here's my hand, prethee thy business?

Elder Lo. Good Sir excuse me, and whatsoever you hear, think must have been known unto you, and be your self discreet, and bear it nobly.

Young Lo. Prethee dispatch me.

Elder Lo. Your Brother's dead Sir.

Young Lo. Thou dost not mean dead drunk?

Elder Lo. No, no, dead and drown'd at sea Sir.

Young Lo. Art sure he's dead?

Elder Lo. Too sure Sir.

Young Lo. I but art thou very certainly sure of it?

Elder Lo. As sure Sir, as I tell it.

Young Lo. But art thou sure he came not up again?

Elder Lo. He may come up, but ne're to call you Brother.

Young Lo. But art sure he had water enough to drown him?

Elder Lo. Sure Sir, he wanted none.

Young Lo. I would not have him want, I lov'd him better; here I forgive thee: and i'faith be plain, how do I bear it?

Elder Lo. Very wisely Sir.

Young Lo. Fill him some wine. Thou dost not see me mov'd, these transitorie toyes ne're trouble me, he's in a better place, my friend I know't. Some fellows would have cryed now, and have curst thee, and faln out with their meat, and kept a pudder; but all this helps not, he was too good for us, and let God keep him: there's the right use on't friend. Off with thy drink, thou hast a spice of sorrow makes thee dry: fill him another. *Savill,* your Master's dead, and who am I now *Savill?* Nay, let's all bear it well, wipe *Savill* wipe, tears are but thrown away: we shall have wenches now, shall we not *Savill?*

Savill. Yes Sir.

Young Lo. And drink innumerable.

Savil. Yes forsooth.

Young Lo. And you'll strain curtsie and be drunk a little?

Savil. I would be glad, Sir, to doe my weak endeavour.

Yo. Lo. You may be brought in time to love a wench too.

Savil In time the sturdie Oak Sir.

Young Lo. Some more wine for my friend there.

Elder Lo. I shall be drunk anon for my good news: but I have a loving Brother, that's my comfort.

Youn[g] Lo. Here's to you Sir, this is the worst I wish you for your news: and if I had another elder Brother, and say it were his chance to feed Haddocks, I should be still the same you see me now, a poor contented Gentleman. More wine for my friend there, he's dry again.

Elder Lo. I shall be if I follow this beginning. Well my dear Brother, if I scape this drowning, 'tis your turn next to sink, you shall duck twice before I help you. Sir I cannot drink more; pray let me have your pardon.

Young Lo. O Lord Sir, 'tis your modestie: more wine, give him a bigger glass; hug him my Captain, thou shalt be my chief mourner.

Capt. And this my pennon: Sir, a full carouse to you, and to my Lord of Land here.

Elder Lo. I feel a buzzing in my brains, pray God they bear this out, and I'le ne're trouble them so far again. Here's to you Sir.

Young Lo. To my dear Steward, down o' your knees you infidel, you Pagan; be drunk and penitent.

Savil. Forgive me Sir, and I'le be any thing.

Young Lo. Then be a Baud, I'le have thee a brave Baud.

Elder Lo. Sir, I must take my leave of you, my business is so urgent.

Young Lo. Let's have a bridling cast before you go. Fill's a new stoupe.

Elder Lo. I dare not Sir, by no means.

Young Lo. Have you any mind to a wench? I would fain gratifie you for the pains you took Sir.

Elder Lo. As little as to the t'other.

Young Lo. If you find any stirring do but say so.

Elder Lo. Sir, you are too bounteous, when I feel that itching, you shall asswage it Sir, before another: this only and Farewell Sir. Your Brother when the storm was most extream, told all about him, he left a will which lies close behind a Chimney in the matted Chamber: and so as well Sir, as you have made me able, I take my leave.

Young Lo. Let us imbrace him all: if you grow drie before you end your business, pray take a baite here, I have a fresh hogshead for you.

Savil. You shall neither will nor chuse Sir. My Master is a wonderfull fine Gentleman, has a fine state, a very fine state Sir, I am his Steward Sir, and his man.

Elder Lo. Would you were your own sir, as I left you. Well I must cast about, or all sinks.

Savil. Farewell Gentleman, Gentleman, Gentleman.

Elder Lo. What would you with me sir?

Savil. Farewell Gentleman.

Elder Lo. O sleep Sir, sleep. [*Exit* Elder Lo.

Young Lo. Well boyes, you see what's faln, let's in and drink, and give thanks for it.

Capt. Let's give thanks for it.

Young Lo. Drunk as I live.

Savil. Drunk as I live boyes.

Young Lo. Why, now thou art able to discharge thine office, and cast up a reckoning of some weight; I will be knighted, for my state will bear it, 'tis sixteen hundred boyes: off with your husks, I'le skin you all in Sattin.

Capt. O sweet *Loveless*!

Savil. All in Sattin? O sweet *Loveless*!

Young Lo. March in my noble Compeeres: and this my Countess shall be led by two: and so proceed we to the Will. [*Exeunt.*

Enter Morecraft *the* Usurer, *and* Widow.

Morec. And Widow as I say be your own friend: your husband left you wealthy, I and wise, continue so sweet duck, continue so. Take heed of young smooth Varlets, younger Brothers: they are worms that will eat through your bags: they are very Lightning, that with a flash or two will melt your money, and never singe your purse-strings: they are Colts, wench Colts, heady and dangerous, till we take 'em up, and make 'em fit for Bonds: look upon me, I have had, and have yet matter of moment girle, matter of moment; you may meet with a worse back, I'le not commend it.

Wid. Nor I neither Sir.

Mor. Yet thus far by your favour Widow, 'tis tuffe.

Wid. And therefore not for my dyet, for I love a tender one.

Mor. Sweet Widow leave your frumps, and be edified: you know my state, I sell no Perspectives, Scarfs, Gloves, nor Hangers, nor put my trust in Shoe-ties; and where your Husband in an age was rising by burnt figs, dreg'd with meal and powdered sugar, saunders, and grains, wormeseed and rotten Raisins, and such vile Tobacco, that made the footmen mangie; I in a year have put up hundreds inclos'd, my Widow, those pleasant Meadows, by a forfeit morgage: for which the poor Knight takes a lone chamber, owes for his Ale, and dare not beat his Hostess: nay more —

Wid. Good Sir no more, what ere my Husband was, I know what I am, and if you marry me, you must bear it bravely off Sir.

Mor. Not with the head, sweet Widow.

Wid. No sweet Sir, but with your shoulders: I must have you dub'd, for under that I will not stoop a feather. My husband was a fellow lov'd to toyle, fed ill, made gain his exercise, and so grew costive, which for that I was his wife, I gave way to, and spun mine own smocks course, and sir, so little: but let that pass, time, that wears all things out, wore out this husband, who in penitence of such fruitless five years marriage, left me great with his wealth, which if you'le be a worthie gossip to, be knighted Sir. [*Enter* Savil.

Morec. Now, Sir, from whom come you? whose man are you Sir?

Savil. Sir, I come from young Master *Loveless.*

Mor. Be silent Sir, I have no money, not a penny for you, he's sunk, your Master's sunk, a perisht man Sir.

Savil. Indeed his Brother's sunk sir, God be with him, a perisht man indeed, and drown'd at Sea.

Morec. How saidst thou, good my friend, his Brother drown'd?

Savil. Untimely sir, at Sea.

Morec. And thy young Master left sole Heir?

Savil. Yes Sir.

Morec. And he wants money?

Sav. Yes, and sent me to you, for he is now to be knighted.

Mor. Widow be wise, there's more Land coming, widow be very wise, and give thanks for me widow.

Widow. Be you very wise, and be knighted, and then give thanks for me Sir.

Savil. What sayes your worship to this mony?

Mor. I say he may have mony if he please.

Savil. A thousand Sir?

Mor. A thousand Sir, provided any wise Sir, his Land lye for the payment, otherwise—

Enter Young Loveless *and* Comrades *to them.*

Savil. He's here himself Sir, and can better tell you.

Mor. My notable dear friend, and worthy Master *Loveless*, and now right worshipfull, all joy and welcom.

Yo. Lo. Thanks to my dear incloser Master *Morecraft*, prethee old Angel gold, salute my family, I'le do as much for yours; this, and your own desires, fair Gentlewoman.

Wid. And yours Sir, if you mean well; 'tis a hansome Gentleman.

Young Lo. Sirrah, my Brother's dead.

More. Dead?

Yo. Lo. Dead, and by this time soust for Ember Weck.

Morecraft. Dead?

Young Lo. Drown'd, drown'd at sea man, by the next fresh Conger that comes we shall hear more.

Mor. Now by my faith of my body it moves me much.

Yo. Lo. What, wilt thou be an Ass, and weep for the dead? why I thought nothing but a general inundation would have mov'd thee, prethe be quiet, he hath left his land behind him.

Morecraft. O has he so?

Young Lo. Yes faith, I thank him for't, I have all boy, hast any ready mony?

Morecraft. Will you sell Sir?

Young Lo. No not out right good Gripe; marry, a morgage or such a slight securitie.

More. I have no mony, Sir, for Morgage; if you will sell, and all or none, I'le work a new Mine for you.

Sav. Good Sir look before you, he'l work you out of all else: if you sell all your Land, you have sold your Country, and then you must to Sea, to seek your Brother, and there lye pickled in a Powdering tub, and break your teeth with Biskets and hard Beef, that must have watering Sir: and where's your 300 pounds a year in drink then? If you'l tun up the Straights you may, for you have no calling for drink there, but with a Canon, nor no scoring but on your Ships sides, and then if you scape with life, and take a Faggot boat and a bottle of *Usquebaugh,* come home poor men, like a tipe of Thames-street stinking of Pitch and Poor-John. I cannot tell Sir, I would be loth to see it.

Capt. Steward, you are an Ass, a meazel'd mungril, and were it not again the peace of my soveraign friend here, I would break your fore-casting Coxcomb, dog I would even with my staffe of Office there. Thy Pen and Inkhorn Noble boy, the God of gold here has fed thee well, take mony for thy durt: hark and believe, thou art cold of constitution, thy eat unhealthful, sell and be wise; we are three that will adorn thee, and live according to thine own heart child; mirth shall be only ours, and only ours shall be the black eyed beauties of the time. Mony makes men Eternal.

Poet. Do what you will, 'tis the noblest course, then you may live without the charge of people, only we four will make a Family, I and an Age that will beget new *Annals,* in which I'le write thy life my son of pleasure, equal with *Nero* and *Caligula.*

Young Lo. What men were they Captain?

Capt. Two roaring Boys of *Rome,* that made all split.

Young Lo. Come Sir, what dare you give?

Sav. You will not sell Sir?

Young Lo. Who told you so Sir?

Sav. Good Sir have a care.

Young Lo. Peace, or I'le tack your Tongue up to your Roof. What money? speak.

More. Six thousand pound Sir.

Capt. Take it, h'as overbidden by the Sun: bind him to his bargain quickly.

Young Lo. Come strike me luck with earnest, and draw the writings.

More. There's a Gods peny for thee.

Sav. Sir for my old Masters sake let my Farm be excepted, if I become his Tenant I am undone, my Children beggers, and my Wife God knows what: consider me dear Sir.

More. I'le have all or none.

Young Lo. All in, all in: dispatch the writings. [*Exit with Com.*

Wid. Go, thou art a pretty forehanded fellow, would thou wert wiser.

Sav. Now do I sensibly begin to feel my self a Rascal; would I could teach a School, or beg, or lye well, I am utterly undone; now he that taught thee to deceive and cousen, take thee to his mercy; so be it.

[*Exit* Savil.

More. Come Widow come, never stand upon a Knight-hood, 'tis a meer paper honour, and not proof enough for a Serjeant. Come, Come, I'le make thee —

Wid. To answer in short, 'tis this Sir. No Knight no Widow, if you make me any thing, it must be a Lady, and so I take my leave.

More. Farewel sweet Widow, and think of it.

Wid. Sir, I do more than think of it, it makes me dream Sir. [*Ex.* Wid.

More. She's rich and sober, if this itch were from her: and say I be at the charge to pay the Footmen, and the Trumpets, I and the Horsemen too, and be a Knight, and she refuse me then; then am I hoist into the subsidy, and so by consequence should prove a Coxcomb: I'le have a care of that. Six thousand pound, and then the Land is mine, there's some refreshing yet. [*Exit.*

Actus Tertius. Scena Prima.

Enter Abigal, *and drops her Glove.*

Abigal. If he but follow me, as all my hopes tell me, he's man enough, up goes my rest, and I know I shall draw him.

Enter Welford.

Wel. This is the strangest pampered piece of flesh towards fifty, that ever frailty copt withal, what a trim *lennoy* here she has put upon me; these women are a proud kind of Cattel, and love this whorson doing so directly, that they will not stick to make their very skins Bawdes to their flesh. Here's Dogskin and Storax sufficient to kill a Hawk: what to do with it, besides nailing it up amongst *Irish* heads of Teere, to shew the mightiness of her Palm, I know not: there she is. I must enter into Dialogue. Lady you have lost your Glove.

Abig. Not Sir, if you have found it.

Wel. It was my meaning Lady to restore it.

Abig. 'Twill be uncivil in me to take back a favour, Fortune hath so well bestowed Sir, pray wear it for me.

Wel. I had rather wear a Bell. But hark you Mistres, what hidden vertue is there in this Glove, that you would have me wear it? Is't good against sore eyes, or will it charm the Toothach? Or these red tops; being steept in white wine soluble, wil't kill the Itch? Or has it so conceal'd a providence to keep my hand from Bonds? If it have none of these and prove no more but a bare Glove of half a Crown a pair, 'twill be but half a courtesie, I wear two alwayes, faith let's draw cuts, one will do me no pleasure.

Abig. The tenderness of his years keeps him as yet in ignorance, he's a well moulded fellow, and I wonder his bloud should stir no higher; but 'tis his want of company: I must grow nearer to him.

Enter Elder Loveless *disguised.*

Elder Lo. God save you both.

Abig. And pardon you Sir; this is somewhat rude, how came you hither?

Elder Lo. Why through the doors, they are open.

Wel. What are you? And what business have you here?

Elder Lo. More I believe than you have.

Abig. Who would this fellow speak with? Art thou sober?

Elder Lo. Yes, I come not here to sleep.

Wel. Prethee what art thou?

Elder Lo. As much (gay man) as thou art, I am a Gentleman.

Wel. Art thou no more?

Elder Lo. Yes more than thou dar'st be; a Souldier.

Abig. Thou dost not come to quarrel?

Elder Lo. No, not with women; I come to speak here with a Gentlewoman.

Abig. Why, I am one.

Elder Lo. But not with one so gentle.

Wel. This is a fine fellow.

Elder Lo. Sir, I am not fine yet. I am but new come over, direct me with your ticket to your Taylor, and then I shall be fine Sir. Lady if there be a better of your Sex within this house, say I would see her.

Abig. Why am not I good enough for you Sir?

Elder Lo. Your way you'l be too good, pray end my business. This is another Sutor, O frail Woman!

Wel. This fellow with his bluntness hopes to do more than the long sutes of a thousand could; though he be sowre he's quick, I must not trust him. Sir, this Lady is not to speak with you, she is more serious: you smell as if you were new calkt; go and be hansome, and then you may sit with her Servingmen.

El. Lo. What are you Sir?

Wel. Guess by my outside.

Elder Lo. Then I take you Sir, for some new silken thing wean'd from the Country, that shall (when you come to keep good company) be beaten into better manners. Pray good proud Gentlewoman, help me to your Mistress.

Abig. How many lives hast thou, that thou talk'st thus rudely?

Elder Lo. But one, one, I am neither Cat nor Woman.

Wel. And will that one life, Sir, maintain you ever in such bold sawciness?

Elder Lo. Yes, amongst a Nation of such men as you are, and be no worse for wearing, shall I speak with this Lady?

Abig. No by my troth shall you not.

Elder Lo. I must stay here then?

Wel. That you shall not neither.

Elder Lo. Good fine thing tell me why?

Wel. Good angry thing I'le tell you:
This is no place for such companions,
Such lousie Gentlemen shall find their business
Better i'th' Suburbs, there your strong pitch perfume,
Mingled with lees of Ale, shall reek in fashion:
This is no Thames-street, Sir.

Abig. This Gentleman informs you truly:
Prethee be satisfied, and seek the Suburbs,
Good Captain, or what ever title else,
The Warlike Eele-boats have bestowed upon thee,
Go and reform thy self, prethee be sweeter,
And know my Lady speaks with no Swabbers.

Elder Lo. You cannot talk me out with your tradition
Of wit you pick from Plays, go to, I have found ye:
And for you, Sir, whose tender gentle blood
Runs in your Nose, and makes you snuff at all,
But three pil'd people, I do let you know,
He that begot your worships Sattin-sute,

Can make no men Sir: I will see this Lady,
And with the reverence of your silkenship,
In these old Ornaments.

Wel. You will not sure?

Elder Lo. Sure Sir I shall.

Abig. You would be beaten out?

Elder Lo. Indeed I would not, or if I would be beaten, Pray who shall beat me? this good Gentleman Looks as if he were o'th' peace.

Wel. Sir you shall see that: will you get you out?

Elder Lo. Yes, that, that shall correct your boys tongue. Dare you fight, I will stay here still. [*They draw.*

Abig. O their things are out, help, help for Gods sake, Madam; Jesus they foin at one another.

Enter Lady.

Madam, why, who is within there?

Lady. Who breeds this rudeness?

Wel. This uncivil fellow; He saies he comes from Sea, where I believe, H'as purg'd away his manners.

Lady. Why what of him?

Wel. Why he will rudely without once God bless you,
Press to your privacies, and no denial
Must stand betwixt your person and his business;
I let go his ill Language.

Lady. Sir, have you business with me?

Elder Lo. Madam some I have,
But not so serious to pawn my life for't:
If you keep this quarter, and maintain about you
Such Knights o'th' *Sun* as this is, to defie
Men of imployment to ye, you may live,

But in what fame?

Lady. Pray stay Sir, who has wrong'd you?

Elder Lo. Wrong me he cannot, though uncivilly
He flung his wild words at me: but to you
I think he did no honour, to deny
The hast I come withal, a passage to you,
Though I seem course.

Lady. Excuse me gentle Sir, 'twas from my knowledge,
And shall have no protection. And to you Sir,
You have shew'd more heat than wit, and from your self
Have borrowed power, I never gave you here,
To do these vile unmanly things: my house
Is no blind street to swagger in; and my favours
Not doting yet on your unknown deserts
So far, that I should make you Master of my business;
My credit yet stands fairer with the people
Than to be tried with swords; and they that come
To do me service, must not think to win me
With hazard of a murther; if your love
Consist in fury, carry it to the Camp:
And there in honour of some common Mistress,
Shorten your youth, I pray be better temper'd:
And give me leave a while Sir.

Wel. You must have it. [*Exit* Welford.

Lady. Now Sir, your business?

El. Lo. First, I thank you for schooling this young fellow,
Whom his own follies, which he's prone enough
Daily to fall into, if you but frown,
Shall level him a way to his repentance:
Next, I should rail at you, but you are a Woman,
And anger's lost upon you.

Lady. Why at me Sir? I never did you wrong, for to my knowledge
This is the first sight of you.

Elder Lo. You have done that,
I must confess I have the least curse in
Because the least acquaintance: But there be
(If there be honour in the minds of men)
Thousands when they shall know what I deliver,
(As all good men must share in't) will to shame
Blast your black memory.

Lady. How is this good Sir?

Elder Lo. 'Tis that, that if you have a soul will choak it: Y'ave kill'd
a Gentleman.

Lady. I kill'd a Gentleman!

Elder Lo. You and your cruelty have kill'd him Woman,
And such a man (let me be angry in't)
Whose least worth weighed above all womens vertues
That are; I spare you all to come too: guess him now?

Lady. I am so innocent I cannot Sir.

Elder Lo. Repent you mean, you are a perfect Woman, And as the
first was, made for mans undoing.

Lady. Sir, you have mist your way, I am not she.

Elder Lo. Would he had mist his way too, though he had Wande-
red farther than Women are ill spoken of, So he had mist this misery, you Lady.

Lady. How do you do, Sir?

Elder Lo. Well enough I hope. While I can keep my self out from
temptations.

Lady. Leap into this matter, whither would ye?

Elder Lo. You had a Servant that your peevishness Injoined to
Travel.

Lady. Such a one I have Still, and shall be griev'd 'twere otherwise.

El. Lo. Then have your asking, and be griev'd he's dead;
How you will answer for his worth, I know not,
But this I am sure, either he, or you, or both
Were stark mad, else he might have liv'd
To have given a stronger testimony to th' world
Of what he might have been. He was a man
I knew but in his evening, ten Suns after,
Forc'd by a Tyrant storm our beaten Bark
Bulg'd under us; in which sad parting blow,
He call'd upon his Saint, but not for life,
On you unhappy Woman, and whilest all
Sought to preserve their Souls, he desperately
Imbrac'd a Wave, crying to all that saw it,
If any live, go to my Fate that forc'd me
To this untimely end, and make her happy:
His name was *Loveless*: And I scap't the storm,
And now you have my business.

Lady. 'Tis too much.
Would I had been that storm, he had not perisht.
If you'l rail now I will forgive you Sir.
Or if you'l call in more, if any more
Come from this ruine, I shall justly suffer
What they can say, I do confess my self
A guiltie cause in this. I would say more,
But grief is grown too great to be delivered.

Elder Lo. I like this well: these women are strange things.
'Tis somewhat of the latest now to weep,
You should have wept when he was going from you,
And chain'd him with those tears at home.

    La. Would you had told me then so, these two arms had been his
Sea.

    Elder Lo. Trust me you move me much: but say he lived, these we-
re forgotten things again.

Lady. I, say you so? Sure I should know that voice: this is knavery. I'le fit you for it. Were he living Sir, I would perswade you to be charitable, I, and confess we are not all so ill as your opinion holds us. O my friend, what penance shall I pull upon my fault, upon my most unworthy self for this?

Elder Lo. Leave to love others, 'twas some jealousie That turn'd him desperate.

Lady. I'le be with you straight: are you wrung there?

Elder Lo. This works amain upon her.

Lady. I do confess there is a Gentleman Has born me long good will.

Elder Lo. I do not like that.

Lady. And vow'd a thousand services to me; to me, regardless of him: But since Fate, that no power can withstand, has taken from me my first, and best love, and to weep away my youth is a mere folly, I will shew you what I determine sir: you shall know all: Call M. *Welford* there: That Gentleman I mean to make the model of my Fortunes, and in his chast imbraces keep alive the memory of my lost lovely *Loveless*: he is somewhat like him too.

Elder Lo. Then you can love.

Lady. Yes certainly Sir? Though it please you to think me hard and cruel, I hope I shall perswade you otherwise.

Elder Lo. I have made my self a fine fool.

Enter Welford.

Wel. Would you have spoke with me Madam?

Lady. Yes M. *Welford,* and I ask your pardon before this Gentleman for being froward: this kiss, and henceforth more affection.

Elder Lo. So, 'tis better I were drown'd indeed.

Wel. This is a sudden passion, God hold it. This fellow out of his fear sure has Perswaded her. I'le give him a new suit on't.

La. A parting kiss, and good Sir, let me pray you To wait me in the Gallerie.

Wel. I am in another world, Madam where you please. [*Exit* Welford.

Elder Lo. I will to Sea, and 't shall goe hard but I'le be drown'd indeed.

La. Now Sir you see I am no such hard creature, But time may win me.

Elder Lo. You have forgot your lost Love.

La. Alas Sir, what would you have me do? I cannot call him back again with sorrow; I'le love this man as dearly, and beshrow me I'le keep him far enough from Sea, and 'twas told me, now I remember me, by an old wise woman, that my first Love should be drown'd, and see 'tis come about.

Elder Lo. I would she had told you your second should be hang'd too, and let that come about: but this is very strange.

La. Faith Sir, consider all, and then I know you'le be of my mind: if weeping would redeem him, I would weep still.

Elder Lo. But say that I were *Loveless*, And scap'd the storm, how would you answer this?

Lady. Why for that Gentleman I would leave all the world.

Elder Lo. This young thing too?

Lady. That young thing too, Or any young thing else: why, I would lose my state.

Elder Lo. Why then he lives still, I am he, your *Loveless*.

Lady. Alas I knew it Sir, and for that purpose prepared this Pageant: get you to your task. And leave these Players tricks, or I shall leave you, indeed I shall. Travel, or know me not.

Elder Lo. Will you then marry?

Lady. I will not promise, take your choice. Farewell.

Elder Lo. There is no other Purgatorie but a Woman. I must doe something. [*Exit* Loveless.

Enter Welford.

Wel. Mistress I am bold.

Lady. You are indeed.

Wel. You so overjoyed me Lady.

Lady. Take heed you surfeit not, pray fast and welcom.

Wel. By this light you love me extreamly.

Lady. By this, and to morrows light, I care not for you.

Wel. Come, come, you cannot hide it.

Lady. Indeed I can, where you shall never find it.

Wel. I like this mirth well Lady.

Lady. You shall have more on't.

Wel. I must kiss you.

Lady. No Sir.

Wel. Indeed I must.

Lady. What must be, must be; I'le take my leave, you have your parting blow: I pray commend me to those few friends you have, that sent you hither, and tell them when you travel next, 'twere fit you brought less bravery with you, and more wit, you'le never get a wife else.

Wel. Are you in earnest?

Lady. Yes faith. Will you eat Sir, your horses will be readie straight, you shall have a napkin laid in the butterie for ye.

Wel. Do not you love me then?

Lady. Yes, for that face.

Wel. It is a good one Ladie.

Lady. Yes, if it were not warpt, the fire in time may mend it.

Wel. Me thinks yours is none of the best Ladie.

Lady. No by my troth Sir; yet o' my conscience, You would make shift with it.

Wel. Come pray no more of this.

Lady. I will not: Fare you well. Ho, who's within there? bring out the Gentlemans horses, he's in haste; and set some cold meat on the Table.

Wel. I have too much of that I thank you Ladie: take your Chamber when you please, there goes a black one with you Ladie.

Lady. Farewell young man. [*Exit* Ladie.

Wel. You have made me one, Farewell: and may the curse of a great house fall upon thee, I mean the Butler. The devil and all his works are in these women, would all of my sex were of my mind, I would make 'em a new Lent, and a long one, that flesh might be in more reverence with them.

Enter Abigal to him.

Abig. I am sorry M. *Welford.*

Wel. So am I, that you are here.

Abig. How does my Ladie use you?

Wel. As I would use you, scurvilie.

Abig. I should have been more kind Sir.

Wel. I should have been undone then. Pray leave me, and look to your sweet-meats; hark, your Ladie calls.

Abig. Sir, I shall borrow so much time without offence.

Wel. Y'are nothing but offence, for Gods love leave me.

Abig. 'Tis strange my Ladie should be such a tyrant?

Wel. To send you to me, 'Pray goe stitch, good doe, y'are more trouble to me than a Term.

Abig. I do not know how my good will, if I said love I lied not, should any way deserve this?

Wel. A thousand waies, a thousand waies; sweet creature let me depart in peace.

Abig. What Creature Sir? I hope I am a woman.

Wel. A hundred I think by your noise.

Abig. Since you are angrie Sir, I am bold to tell you that I am a woman, and a rib.

Wel. Of a roasted horse.

Abig. Conster me that?

Wel. A Dog can doe it better; Farwell Countess, and commend me to your Ladie, tell her she's proud, and scurvie, and so I commit you both to your tempter.

Abig. Sweet Mr. *Welford.*

Wel. Avoid old Satanus: Go daub your ruines, your face looks fouler than a storm: the Foot-man stayes for you in the Lobby Lady.

Abig. If you were a Gentleman, I should know it by your gentle conditions: are these fit words to give a Gentlewoman?

Wel. As fit as they were made for ye: Sirrah, my horses. Farwell old Adage, keep your nose warm, the Rheum will make it horn else— [*Exit* Welford.

Abig. The blessings of a Prodigal young heir be thy companions *Welford*, marry come up my Gentleman, are your gums grown so tender they cannot bite? A skittish Filly will be your fortune *Welford*, and fair enough for such a packsaddle. And I doubt not (if my aim hold) to see her made to amble to your hand. [*Exit Abigal.*

Enter Young Loveless, *and* Comrades, Morecraft, Widow, Savil, *and the rest.*

Captain. Save thy brave shoulder, my young puissant Knight, and may thy back Sword bite them to the bone that love thee not, thou art an errant man, go on. The circumcis'd shall fall by thee. Let Land and labour fill the man that tills, thy sword must be thy plough, and *Jove* it speed. *Mecha* shall sweat, and *Mahomet* shall fall, and thy dear name fill up his monument.

Yo. L. It shall Captain, I mean to be a Worthy.

Cap. One Worthy is too little, thou shalt be all.

Mor. Captain I shall deserve some of your love too.

Capt. Thou shalt have heart and hand too, noble *Morecraft*, if them wilt lend me mony. I am a man of Garrison, be rul'd, and open to me those infernal gates, whence none of thy evil Angels pass again, and I will stile thee noble, nay *Don Diego*. I'le woo thy *Infanta* for thee, and my Knight shall feast her with high meats, and make her apt.

Mor. Pardon me Captain, y'are beside my meaning.

Young Lo. No Mr. *Morecraft*, 'tis the Captains meaning I should prepare her for ye.

Capt. Or provok her. Speak my modern man, I say provoke her.

Poet. Captain, I say so too, or stir her to it. So say the Criticks.

Young Lo. But howsoever you expound it sir, she's very welcom, and this shall serve for witness. And Widow, since y'are come so happily, you shall deliver up the keyes, and free possession of this house, whilst I stand by to ratifie.

Wid. I had rather give it back again believe me, 'Tis a miserie to say you had it. Take heed?

Young Lo. 'Tis past that Widow, come, sit down, some wine there, there is a scurvie banquet if we had it. All this fair house is yours Sir *Savil*?

Savil. Yes Sir.

Young Lo. Are your keyes readie, I must ease your burden.

Sav. I am readie Sir to be undone, when you shall call me to't.

Young Lo. Come come, thou shalt live better.

Sav. I shall have less to doe, that's all, there's half a dozen of my friends i'th' fields sunning against a bank, with half a breech among 'em, I shall be with 'em shortly. The care and continuall vexation of being rich, eat up this rascall. What shall become of my poor familie, they are no sheep, and they must keep themselves.

Young Lo. Drink Master *Morecraft*, pray be merrie all: Nay and you will not drink there's no societie, Captain speak loud, and drink: widow, a word.

Cap. Expou[n]d her throughly Knight. Here God o' gold, here's to thy fair possessions; Be a Baron and a bold one: leave off your tickling of young heirs like Trouts, and let thy Chimnies smoke. Feed men of war, live and be honest, and be saved yet.

Mor. I thank you worthie Captain for your counsel. You keep y-our Chimnies smoking there, your nostrils, and when you can, you feed a man of War, this makes you not a Baron, but a bare one: and how or when you shall be saved, let the Clark o'th' companie (you have commanded) have a just care of.

Poet. The man is much moved. Be not angrie Sir, but as the Poet sings, let your displeasure be a short furie, and goe out. You have spoke home, and bitterly, to me Sir. Captain take truce, the Miser is a tart and a wittie whorson —

Cap. Poet, you feign perdie, the wit of this man lies in his fingers ends, he must tell all; his tongue fills his mouth like a neats tongue, and only serves to lick his hungrie chaps after a purchase: his brains and brimstone are the devils diet to a fat usurers head: To her Knight, to her: clap her aboard, and stow her. Where's the brave Steward?

Savil. Here's your poor friend, and *Savil* Sir.

Capt. Away, th'art rich in ornaments of nature. First in thy face, thou hast a serious face, a betting, bargaining, and saving face, a rich face, pawn it to the Usurer; a face to kindle the compassion of the most ignorant and frozen Justice.

Savil. 'Tis such I dare not shew it shortly sir.

Capt. Be blithe and bonny steward: Master *Morecraft*, Drink to this man of reckoning?

Mor. Here's e'ne to him.

Savil. The Devil guide it downward: would there were in't an acre of the great broom field he bought, to sweep your durtie Conscience, or to choak ye, 'tis all one to me, Usurer.

Young Lo. Consider what I told you, you are young, unapt for worldly business: Is it fit one of such tenderness, so delicate, so contrarie to things of care, should stir and break her better meditati-ons, in the bare brokage of a brace of Angels? or a new Kirtel, though it be Satten? eat by the hope of surfeits, and lie down only in expectation of a morrow, that may undo some easie hearted fool, or reach a widows curses? Let out mony, whose use returns the principal? and get out of these troubles, a consuming heir: For such a one must follow necessarily, you shall die hated, if not old and miserable; and that possest wealth that you got with pining, live to see tumbled to anothers hands, that is no more a kin to you, than you to his couzenage.

Widow. Sir you speak well, would God that charity had first begun here.

Young Lo. 'Tis yet time. Be merrie, me thinks you want wine there, there's more i'th' house. Captain, where rests the health?

Captain. It shall goe round boy.

Young Lo. Say you can suffer this, because the end points at much profit, can you so far bow below your blood, below your too much beautie, to be a partner of this fellowes bed, and lie with his diseases? if you can, I will no[t] press you further: yet look upon him: there's nothing in that hide-bound Usurer, that man of mat, that all decai'd, but aches, for you to love, unless his perisht lungs, his drie cough, or his scurvie. This is truth, and so far I dare speak yet: he has yet past cure of Physick, spaw, or any diet, a primitive pox in his bones; and o' my Knowledge he has been ten times rowell'd: ye may love him; he had a bastard, his own toward issue, whipt, and then cropt for washing out the roses, in three farthings to make 'em pence.

Widow. I do not like these Morals.

Young Lo. You must not like him then.

Enter Elder Love.

Elder Lo. By your leave Gentlemen?

Young Lo. By my troth sir you are welcom, welcom faith: Lord what a stranger you are grown; pray know this Gentlewoman, and if you please these friends here: we are merry, you see the worst on't; your house has been kept warm Sir.

Elder Lo. I am glad to hear it Brother, pray God you are wise too.

Young Lo. Pray Mr. *Morecraft* know my elder Brother, and Captain do you complement. *Savil* I dare swear is glad at heart to see you;

Lord, we heard Sir you were drown'd at Sea, and see how luckily things come about!

More. This mony must be paid again Sir.

Young Lo. No Sir, pray keep the Sale, 'twill make good Tailors measures; I am well I thank you.

Wid. By my troth the Gentleman has stew'd him in his own Sawce, I shall love him for't.

Sav. I know not where I am, I am so glad: your worship is the welcom'st man alive; upon my knees I bid you welcome home: here has been such a hurry, such a din, such dismal Drinking, Swearing and Whoring, 'thas almost made me mad: we have all liv'd in a continual *Turnbal-street*; Sir, blest be Heaven, that sent you safe again, now shall I eat and go to bed again.

Elder Lo. Brother dismiss these people.

Young Lo. Captain be gone a while, meet me at my old *Randevouse* in the evening, take your small Poet with you. Mr. *Morecraft* you were best go prattle with your learned Counsel, I shall preserve your mony, I was couzen'd when time was, we are quit Sir.

Wid. Better and better still.

Elder Lo. What is this fellow, Brother?

Young Lo. The thirsty Usurer that supt my Land off.

Elder Lo. What does he tarry for?

Young Lo. Sir to be Landlord of your House and State: I was bold to make a little sale Sir.

More. Am I overreach'd? if there be Law I'le hamper ye.

Elder Lo Prethee be gone, and rave at home, thou art so base a fool I cannot laugh at thee: Sirrah, this comes of couzening, home and spare, eat Reddish till you raise your sums again. If you stir far in this, I'le have you whipt, your ears nail'd for intelligencing o'the Pillory, and your goods forfeit: you are a stale couzener, leave my house: no more.

More. A pox upon your house. Come Widow, I shall yet hamper this young Gamester.

Wid. Good twelve i'th' hundred keep your way, I am not for your diet, marry in your own Tribe *Jew*, and get a Broker.

Young Lo. 'Tis well said Widow: will you jog on Sir?

More. Yes, I will go, but 'tis no matter whither: But when I trust a wild Fool, and a Woman, May I lend Gratis, and build Hospitals.

Young Lo. Nay good Sir, make all even, here's a Widow wants y-our good word for me, she's rich, and may renew me and my fortu-nes.

Elder Lo. I am glad you look before you. Gentlewoman, here is a poor distressed younger Brother.

Wid. You do him wrong Sir, he's a Knight.

Elder Lo. I ask you mercy: yet 'tis no matter, his Knighthood is no inheritance I take it: whatsoever he is, he is your Servant, or would be, Lady. Faith be not merciless, but make a man; he's young and handsome, though he be my Brother, and his observances may de-serve your Love: he shall not fail for means.

Wid. Sir you speak like a worthy Brother: and so much I do credit your fair Language, that I shall love your Brother: and so love him, but I shall blush to say more.

Elder Lo. Stop her mouth. I hope you shall not live to know that hour when this shall be repented. Now Brother I should chide, but I'le give no distaste to your fair Mistress. I will instruct her in't and she shall do't: you have been wild and ignorant, pray mend it.

Young Lo. Sir, every day now Spring comes on.

Elder Lo. To you good Mr. *Savil* and your Office, thus much I have to say: Y'are from my Steward become, first your own Drunkard, then his Bawd: they say y'are excellent grown in both, and perfect: give me your keys Sir *Savil*.

Savil. Good Sir consider whom you left me to.

Elder Lo. I left you as a curb for, not to provoke my Brothers fol-lies: where's the best drink, now? come, tell me *Savil*; where's the soundest Whores? Ye old he Goat, ye dried Ape, ye lame Stallion, must you be leading in my house your Whores, like Fairies dance their night rounds, without fear either of King or Constable, within my walls? Are all my Hangings safe; my Sheep unfold yet? I hope my Plate is currant, I ha' too much on't. What say you to 300 pounds in drink now?

Sav. Good Sir forgive me, and but hear me speak?

Elder Lo. Me thinks thou shouldst be drunk still, and not speak, 'tis the more pardonable.

Sav. I will Sir, if you will have it so.

Elder Lo. I thank ye: yes, e'ne pursue it Sir: do you hear? get a Whore soon for your recreation: go look out Captain *Broken-breech* your fellow, and Quarrel if you dare: I shall deliver these Keys to one shall have more honesty, though not so much fine wit Sir. You may walk and gather *Cresses* fit to cool your Liver; there's something for you to begin a Diet, you'l have the Pox else. Speed you well, Sir *Savil*: you may eat at my house to preserve life; but keep no Fornication in the Stables. [*Ex. om. pr.* Savil.

Sav. Now must I hang my self, my friends will look for't.
Eating and sleeping, I do despise you both now:
I will run mad first, and if that get not pitty,
I'le drown my self, to a most dismal ditty. [*Exit* Savil.

Actus Quartus. Scena Prima.

Enter Abigal *sola.*

Abigal. Alas poor Gentlewoman, to what a misery hath Age brought thee: to what a scurvy Fortune! Thou that hast been a Companion for Noblemen, and at the worst of those times for Gentlemen: now like a broken Servingman, must beg for favour to those, that would have crawl'd like Pilgrims to my Chamber but for an Apparition of me. You that be coming on, make much of fifteen, and so till five and twenty: use your time with reverence, that your profits may arise: it will not tarry with you, *Ecce signum*: here was a face, but time that like a surfeit eats our youth, plague of his iron teeth, and draw 'em for't, has been a little bolder here than welcome: and now to say the truth, I am fit for no man. Old men i'th' house of fifty, call me Granum; and when they are drunk, e'ne then, when *Jone* and my Lady are all one, not one will do me reason. My little Levite hath forsaken me, his silver sound of Cittern quite abolish[t], [h]is doleful *hymns* under my Chamber window, digested into tedious learning: well fool, you leapt a Haddock when you left him: he's a clean man, and a good edifier, and twenty nobles is his state *de claro*, besides his pigs in *posse*. To this good *Homilist* I have been ever stubborn, which God forgive me for, and mend my manners: and Love, if ever thou hadst care of forty, of such a piece of lape ground, hear my prayer, and fire his zeal so far forth that my faults in this renued impression of my love may shew corrected to our gentle reader.

Enter Roger.

See how negligently he passes by me: with what an Equipage Canonical, as though he had broken the heart of *Bellarmine*, or added something to the singing Brethren. 'Tis scorn, I know it, and deserve it, Mr. *Roger*.

Rog. Fair Gentlewoman, my name is *Roger*.

Abig. Then gentle *Roger*?

Rog. Ungentle *Abigal.*

Abig. Why M'r *Roger* will you set your wit to a weak womans?

Rog. You are weak indeed: for so the Poet sings.

Abig. I do confess my weakness, sweet Sir *Roger.*

Rog. Good my Ladies Gentlewoman, or my good Ladies Gentlewoman (this trope is lost to you now) leave your prating, you have a season of your first mother in ye: and surely had the Devil been in love, he had been abused too: go *Dalilah*, you make men fools, and wear Fig-breeches.

Abi. Well, well, hard hearted man; dilate upon the weak infirmities of women: these are fit texts, but once there was a time, would I had never seen those eyes, those eyes, those orient eyes.

Rog. I they were pearls once with you.

Abi. Saving your reverence Sir, so they are still.

Rog. Nay, nay, I do beseech you leave your cogging, what they are, they are, they serve me without Spectacles I thank 'em.

Abig. O will you kill me?

Rog. I do not think I can, Y'are like a Copy-hold with nine lives in't.

Abig. You were wont to bear a Christian fear about you: For your own worships sake.

Rog. I was a Christian fool then: Do you remember what a dance you led me? how I grew qualm'd in love, and was a dunce? could expound but once a quarter, and then was out too: and then out of the stinking stir you put me in, I prayed for my own issue. You do remember all this?

Abig. O be as then you were!

Rog. I thank you for it, surely I will be wiser *Abigal*: and as the Ethnick Poet sings, I will not lose my oyl and labour too. Y'are for the worshipfull I take it *Abigal*.

Abig. O take it so, and then I am for thee!

Rog. I like these tears well, and this humbling also, they are Symptomes of contrition. If I should fall into my fit again, would you not shake me into a quotidian Coxcombe? Would you not use me scurvily again, and give me possets with purging Confets in't? I tell thee Gentlewoman, thou hast been harder to me, than a long pedigree.

Abig. O Curate cure me: I will love thee better, dearer, longer: I will do any thing, betray the secrets of the main house-hold to thy reformation. My Ladie shall look lovingly on thy learning, and when true time shall point thee for a Parson, I will convert thy egges to penny custards, and thy tith goose shall graze and multiply.

Rog. I am mollified, as well shall testifie this faithfull kiss, and have a great care Mistris *Abigal* how you depress the Spirit any more with your rebukes and mocks: for certainly the edge of such a follie cuts it self.

Abigal. O Sir, you have pierc'd me thorow. Here I vow a recantation to those malicious faults I ever did against you. Never more will I despise your learning, never more pin cards and cony tails upon your Cassock, never again reproach your reverend nightcap, and call it by the mangie name of murrin, never your reverend person more, and say, you look like one of *Baals* Priests in a hanging, never again when you say grace laugh at you, nor put you out at prayers: never cramp you more, nor when you ride, get Sope and Thistles for you. No my *Roger*, these faults shall be corrected and amended, as by the tenour of my tears appears.

Rog. Now cannot I hold if I should be hang'd, I must crie too. Come to thine own beloved, and do even what thou wilt with me sweet, sweet *Abigal*. I am thine own for ever: here's my hand, when *Roger* proves a recreant, hang him i'th' Bel-ropes.

Enter Lady, *and* Martha.

Lady. Why how now Master *Roger*, no prayers down with you to night? Did you hear the bell ring? You are courting: your flock shall fat well for it.

Rog. I humbly ask your pardon: I'le clap up Prayers, but stay a little, and be with you again. [*Exit* Roger.

Enter Elder Love.

Lady. How dare you, being so unworthie a fellow, Presume to come to move me any more?

Elder Lo. Ha, ha, ha.

Lady. What ails the fellow?

Elder Lo. The fellow comes to laugh at you, I tell you Ladie I would not for your Land, be such a Coxcomb, such a whining Ass, as you decreed me for when I was last here.

Lady. I joy to hear you are wise, 'tis a rare Jewel In an Elder Brother: pray be wiser yet.

Elder Lo. Me thinks I am very wise: I do not come a wooing. Indeed I'le move no more love to your Ladiship.

Lady. What makes you here then?

Elder Lo. Only to see you and be merry Ladie: that's all my business. Faith let's be very merry. Where's little *Roger*? he's a good fellow: an hour or two well spent in wholesome mirth, is worth a thousand of these puling passions. 'Tis an ill world for Lovers.

Lady. They were never fewer.

Elder Lo. I thank God there's one less for me Ladie.

Lady. You were never any Sir.

Elder Lo. Till now, and now I am the prettiest fellow.

Lady. You talk like a Tailor Sir.

Elder Lo. Me thinks your faces are no such fine things now.

Lady. Why did you tell me you were wise? Lord what a lying age is this, where will you mend these faces?

Elder Lo. A Hogs face soust is worth a hundred of 'em.

Lady. Sure you had a Sow to your Mother.

Elder Lo. She brought such fine white Pigs as you, fit for none but Parsons Ladie.

Lady. 'Tis well you will allow us our Clergie yet.

Elder Lo. That shall not save you. O that I were in love again with a wish.

Lady. By this light you are a scurvie fellow, pray be gone.

Elder Lo. You know I am a clean skin'd man.

Lady. Do I know it?

Elder Lo. Come, come, you would know it; that's as good: but not a snap, never long for't, not a snap dear Ladie.

Lady. Hark ye Sir, hark ye, get ye to the Suburbs, there's horse flesh for such hounds: will you goe Sir?

Elder Lo. Lord how I lov'd this woman, how I worshipt this prettie calf with the white face here: as I live, you were the prettiest fool to play withall, the wittiest little varlet, it would talk: Lord how it talk't! and when I angred it, it would cry out, and scratch, and eat no meat, and it would say, goe hang.

Lady. It will say so still, if you anger it.

Elder Lo. And when I askt it, if it would be married, it sent me of an errand into *France*, and would abuse me, and be glad it did so.

Lady. Sir this is most unmanly, pray by gon.

Elder Lo. And swear (even when it twitter'd to be at me) I was unhansome.

Lady. Have you no manners in you?

Elder Lo. And say my back was melted, when God he knows, I kept it at a charge: Four *Flaunders* Mares would have been easier to me, and a Fencer.

Lady. You think all this is true now?

Elder Lo. Faith whether it be or no, 'tis too good for you. But so much for our mirth: Now have at you in earnest.

L[a]. There is enough Sir, I desire no more.

El. Lo. Yes faith, wee'l have a cast at your best parts now. And then the Devil take the worst.

Lady. Pray Sir no more, I am not so much affected with your commendations, 'tis almost dinner, I know they stay for you at the Ordinary.

Elder Lo. E'ne a short Grace, and then I am gone; You are a woman, and the proudest that ever lov'd a Coach: the scornfullest, scurviest, and most senceless woman; the greediest to be prais'd, and never mov'd though it be gross and open; the most envious, that at the poor fame of anothers face, would eat your own, and more than is your own, the paint belonging to it: of such a self opinion, that you think none can deserve your glove: and for your malice, you are so excellent, you might have been your Tempters tutor: nay, never cry.

Lady. Your own heart knows you wrong me: I cry for ye?

Elder Lo. You shall before I leave you.

Lady. Is all this spoke in earnest?

Elder Lo. Yes and more as soon as I can get it out.

Lady. Well out with't.

Elder Lo. You are, let me see.

Lady. One that has us'd you with too much respect.

Elder Lo. One that hath us'd me (since you will have it so) the basest, the most Foot-boy-like, without respect of what I was, or what you might be by me; you have us'd me, as I would use a jade, ride him off's legs, then turn him to the Commons; you have us'd me with discretion, and I thank ye. If you have many more such pretty Servants, pray build an Hospital, and when they are old, pray keep 'em for shame.

Lady. I cannot think yet this is serious.

Elder Lo. Will you have more on't?

Lady. No faith, there's enough if it be true: Too much by all my part; you are no Lover then?

Elder Lo. No, I had rather be a Carrier.

Lady. Why the Gods amend all.

Elder Lo. Neither do I think there can be such a fellow found i'th' world, to be in love with such a froward woman, if there be such, they're mad, *Jove* comfort 'em. Now you have all, and I as new a man, as light, and spirited, that I feel my self clean through another creature. O 'tis brave to be ones own man, I can see you now as I would see a Picture, sit all day by you and never kiss your hand: hear you sing, and never fall backward: but with as set a temper, as I would hear a Fidler, rise and thank you. I can now keep my mony in my purse, that still was gadding out for Scarfes and Wastcoats: and keep my hand from Mercers sheep-skins finely. I can eat mutton now, and feast my self with my two shillings, and can see a play for eighteen pence again. I can my Ladie.

Lady. The carriage of this fellow vexes me. Sir, pray let me speak a little private with you, I must not suffer this.

Elder Lo. Ha, ha, ha, what would you with me? You will not ravish me? Now, your set speech?

Lady. Thou perjur'd man.

Elder Lo. Ha, ha, ha, this is a fine *exordium.* And why I pray you perjur'd?

Lady. Did you not swear a thousand thousand times you lov'd me best of all things?

Elder Lo. I do confess it: make your best of that.

Lady. Why do you say you do not then?

Elder Lo. Nay I'le swear it, And give sufficient reason, your own usage.

Lady. Do you not love me then?

Elder Lo. No faith.

Lady. Did you ever think I lov'd you dearly?

Elder Lo. Yes, but I see but rotten fruits on't.

Lady. Do not denie your hand for I must kiss it, and take my last farewell, now let me die so you be happy.

El. Lo. I am too foolish: Ladie speak dear Ladie.

Lady. No let me die. *She swounds.*

Mar. Oh my Sister!

Abi. O my Ladie help, help.

Mar. Run for some *Rosalis*!

Elder Lo. I have plaid the fine ass: bend her bodie, Lady, best, dearest, worthiest Lady, hear your Servant, I am not as I shew'd: O wretched fool, to fling away the Jewel of thy life thus. Give her more air, see she begins to stir, sweet Mistress hear me!

Lady. Is my Servant well?

Elder Lo. In being yours I am so.

Lady. Then I care not.

Elder Lo. How do ye, reach a chair there; I confess my fault not pardonable, in pursuing thus upon such tenderness my wilfull error; but had I known it would have wrought thus with ye, thus strangely, not the world had won me to it, and let not (my best Ladie) any word spoke to my end disturb your quiet peace: for sooner shall you know a general ruine, than my faith broken. Do not doubt this Mistris, for by my life I cannot live without you. Come, come, you shall not grieve, rather be angrie, and heap infliction upon me: I will suffer. O I could curse my self, pray smile upon me. Upon my faith it was but a trick to trie you, knowing you lov'd me dearlie, and yet strangely that you would never shew it, though my means was all humilitie.

All. Ha, ha.

Elder Lo. How now?

Lady. I thank you fine fool for your most fine plot; this was a sub-tile one, a stiff device to have caught Dottrels with. Good senceless Sir, could you imagine I should swound for you, and know your self to be an arrant ass? I, a discovered one. 'Tis quit I thank you Sir. Ha, ha, ha.

Mar. Take heed Sir, she may chance to swound again.

All. Ha, ha, ha.

Abi. Step to her Sir, see how she changes colour.

Elder Lo. I'le goe to hell first, and be better welcom. I am fool'd, I do confess it, finely fool'd, Ladie, fool'd Madam, and I thank you for it.

Lady. Faith 'tis not so much worth Sir: But if I knew when you come next a burding, I'le have a stronger noose to hold the Woodcock.

All. Ha, ha, ha.

Elder Lo. I am glad to see you merry, pray laugh on.

Mar. H'ad a hard heart that could not laugh at you Sir, ha, ha, ha.

Lady. Pray Sister do not laugh, you'le anger him,
And then hee'l rail like a rude Costermonger,
That School-boys had couzened of his Apples,
As loud and senceless.

Elder Lo. I will not rail.

Mar. Faith then let's hear him Sister.

Elder Lo. Yes, you shall hear me.

Lady. Shall we be the better by it then?

Eld. L. No, he that makes a woman better by his words, I'le have him Sainted: blows will not doe it.

Lady. By this light hee'll beat us.

Elder Lo. You do deserve it richly, And may live to have a Beadle doe it.

Lady. Now he rails.

Elder Lo. Come scornfull Folly, If this be railing, you shall hear me rail.

Lady. Pray put it in good words then.

Elder Lo. The worst are good enough for such a trifle, Such a proud piece of Cobweblawn.

Lady. You bite Sir?

Elder Lo. I would till the bones crackt, and I had my will.

Mar. We had best muzzel him, he grows mad.

Elder Lo. I would 'twere lawfull in the next great sickness to have the Dogs spared, those harmless creatures, and knock i'th' head these hot continual plagues, women, that are more infectious. I hope the State will think on't.

Lady. Are you well Sir?

Mar. He looks as though he had a grievous fit o'th' Colick.

Elder Lo. Green-ginger will cure me.

Abig. I'le heat a trencher for him.

Elder Lo. Durty *December* doe, Thou with a face as old as *Erra Pater*, such a Prognosticating nose: thou thing that ten years since has left to be a woman, outworn the expectation of a Baud; and thy dry bones can reach at nothing now, but gords or ninepins, pray goe fetch a trencher goe.

Lady. Let him alone, he's crack't.

Abig. I'le see him hang'd first, is a beastly fellow to use a woman of my breeding thus; I marry is he: would I were a man, I'de make him eat his Knaves words!

Elder Lo. Tie your she Otter up, good Lady folly, she stinks worse than a Bear-baiting.

Lady. Why will you be angry now?

Elder Lo. Goe paint and purge, call in your kennel with you: you a Lady?

Abi. Sirra, look to't against the quarter Sessions, if there be good behaviour in the world, I'le have thee bound to it.

Elder Lo. You must not seek it in your Ladies house then; pray send this Ferret home, and spin good *Abigal.* And Madam, that your Ladiship may know, in what base manner you have us'd my service, I do from this hour hate thee heartily; and though your folly should whip you to repentance, and waken you at length to see my wrongs, 'tis not the endeavour of your life shall win me; not all the friends you have, intercession, nor your submissive letters, though they spoke as many tears as words; not your knees grown to th' ground in penitence, nor all your state, to kiss you; nor my pardon, nor will to give you Christian burial, if you dye thus; so farewell. When I am married and made sure, I'le come and visit you again, and vex you Ladie. By all my hopes I'le be a torment to you, worse than a tedious winter. I know you will recant and sue to me, but save that labour: I'le rather love a fever and continual thirst, rather contract my youth to drink and sacerdote upon quarrels, or take a drawn whore from an Hospital, that time, diseases, and *Mercury* had eaten, than to be drawn to love you.

Lady. Ha, ha, ha, pray do, but take heed though.

Elder Lo. From thee, false dice, jades, Cowards, and plaguy Summers, good Lord deliver me. [*Exit* Elder Love.

Lady. But hark you Servant, hark ye: is he gon? call him again.

Abigal. Hang him Paddock.

Lady. Art thou here still? flie, flie, and call my Servant, flie or ne'r see me more.

Abigal. I had rather knit again than see that rascall, but I must doe it. [*Exit* Abigal.

Lady. I would be loth to anger him too much; what fine foolery is this in a woman, to use those men most forwardly they love most? If I should lose him thus, I were rightly served. I hope he's not so much himself, to take it to th'heart: how now? will he come back?

Enter Abigal.

Abig. Never, he swears, whilst he can hear men say there's any woman living: he swore he would ha' me first.

Lady. Didst thou intreat him wench?

Abigal. As well as I could Madam. But this is still your way, to love being absent, and when he's with you, laugh at him and abuse him. There's another way if you could hit on't.

Lady. Thou saist true, get me paper, pen and ink, I'le write to him, I'de be loth he should sleep in's anger. Women are most fools when they think th'are wisest. [*Ex. Omnes.*

Musick. Enter Young Loveless, *and* Widow, *going to be Married, with them his* Comrades.

Widow. Pray Sir cast off these fellows, as unfitting for your bare knowledge, and far more your companie: is't fit such Ragamuffins as these are should bear the name of friends? and furnish out a civil house? ye're to be married now, and men that love you must expect a course far from your old carrier: if you will keep 'em, turn 'em to th' stable, and there make 'em grooms: and yet now consider it, such beggars once set o' horse back, you have heard will ride, how far you had best to look.

Captain. Hear you, you that must be Ladie, pray content your self and think upon your carriage soon at night, what dressing will best take your Knight, what wastcote, what cordial will do well i'th' morning for him, what triers have you?

Widow. What do you mean Sir?

Capt. Those that must switch him up: if he start well, fear not but cry Saint *George*, and bear him hard: when you perceive his wind growes hot and wanting, let him a little down, he's fleet, ne're doubt him, and stands sound.

Widow. Sir, you hear these fellows?

Young Love. Merrie companions, wench, Merry companions.

Widow. To one another let 'em be companions, but good Sir not to you: you shall be civil and slip off these base trappings.

Cap. He shall not need, my most swee[t] Ladie Grocer, if he be civil, not your powdered Sugar, nor your Raisins shall perswade the Captain to live a Coxcomb with him; let him be civil and eat i'th' *Arches*, and see what will come on't.

Poet. Let him be civil, doe: undo him; I, that's the next way. I will not take (if he be civil once) two hundred pound a year to live with him; be civil? there's a trim perswasion.

Capt. If thou beest civil Knight, as *Jove* defends it, get thee another nose, that will be pull'd off by the angry boyes for thy conversion: the children thou shalt get on this Civillian cannot inherit by the law, th'are *Ethnicks*, and all thy sport meer Moral leacherie: when they are grown, having but little in 'em, they may prove Haberdashers, or gross Grocers, like their dear Damm there: prethee be civil Knight, in time thou maist read to thy houshold, and be drunk once a year: this would shew finely.

Young Lo. I wonder sweet heart you will offer this, you do not understand these Gentlemen: I will be short and pithy: I had rather cast you off by the way of charge: these are Creatures, that nothing goes to the maintenance of but Corn and Water. I will keep these fellows just in the competencie of two Hens.

Wid. If you can cast it so Sir, you have my liking. If they eat less, I should not be offended: But how these Sir, can live upon so little as Corn and Water, I am unbelieving.

Young Lo. Why prethee sweet heart what's your Ale? is not that Corn and Water, my sweet Widow?

Wid. I but my sweet Knight where's the meat to this, and cloaths that they must look for?

Young Lo. In this short sentence Ale, is all included: Meat, Drink, and Cloth; These are no ravening Footmen, no fellows, that at Ordinaries dare eat their eighteen pence thrice out before they rise, and yet goe hungry to play, and crack more nuts than would suffice a dozen Squirrels; besides the din, which is damnable: I had rather rail, and be confin'd to a *Boatmaker*, than live amongst such rascals; these are people of such a clean discretion in their diet, of such a moderate sustenance, that they sweat if they but smell hot meat. *Porredge* is poison, they hate a Kitchin as they hate a Counter, and show 'em but a Feather-bed they swound. Ale is their eating and their drinking surely, which keeps their bodies clear, and soluble. Bread is a binder, and for that abolisht even in their Ale, whose lost room fills an apple, which is more airy and of subtiler nature. The rest they take is little, and that little is little easie: For like strict men of order, they do correct their bodies with a bench, or a poor stubborn table; if a chimny offer it self with some few broken rushes, they are in down: when they are sick, that's drunk, they may have fresh straw, else they do despise these worldly pamperings. For their poor apparel, 'tis worn out to the diet; new they seek none, and if a man should offer, they are angrie, scarce to be reconcil'd again with him: you shall not hear 'em ask one a cast doublet once in a year, which is modesty befitting my poor friends: you see their *Wardrobe*, though slender, competent: For shirts I take it, they are things worn out of their remembrance. Lousie they will be when they list, and *mangie*, which shows a fine variety: and then to cure 'em, a *Tanners* limepit, which is little charge, two dogs, and these; these two may be cur'd for 3. pence.

Wid. You have half perswaded me, pray use your pleasure: and my good friends since I do know your diet, I'le take an order, meat shall not offend you, you shall have Ale.

Capt. We ask no more, let it be, mighty Lady: and if we perish, then our own sins on us.

Young Lo. Come forward Gentlemen, to Church my boys, when we have done, I'le give you cheer in bowles. [*Exeunt.*

Actus Quintus. Scena Prima.

Enter Elder Loveless.

Elder Lo. This senseless woman vexes me to th' heart, she will not from my memory: would she were a man for one two hours, that I might beat her. If I had been unhansome, old or jealous, 'thad been an even lay she might have scorn'd me; but to be young, and by this light I think as proper as the proudest; made as clean, as straight, and strong backt; means and manners equal with the best cloth of silver Sir i'th' kingdom: But these are things at some time of the Moon, below the cut of Canvas: sure she has some Meeching Rascal in her house, some Hind, that she hath seen bear (like another *Milo*) quarters of Malt upon his back, and sing with't, Thrash all day, and i'th' evening in his stockings, strike up a Hornpipe, and there stink two hours, and ne're a whit the worse man; these are they, these steel chin'd Rascals that undo us all. Would I had been a Carter, or a Coachman, I had done the deed e're this time.

Enter Servant.

Ser. Sir, there's a Gentleman without would speak with you.

Elder Lo. Bid him come in.

Enter Welford.

Wel. By your leave Sir.

Elder Lo. You are welcome, what's your will Sir?

Wel. Have you forgotten me?

Elder Lo. I do not much remember you.

Wel. You must Sir. I am that Gentleman you pleas'd to wrong, in your disguise, I have inquired you out.

Elder Lo. I was disguised indeed Sir if I wrong'd you, pray where and when?

Wel. In such a Ladies house, I need not name her.

Elder Lo. I do remember you, you seem'd to be a Sutor to that Lady?

Wel. If you remember this, do not forget how scurvily you us'd me: that was no place to quarrel in, pray you think of it; if you be honest you dare fight with me, without more urging, else I must provoke ye.

Elder Lo. Sir I dare fight, but never for a woman, I will not have her in my cause, she's mortal, and so is not my anger: if you have brought a nobler subject for our Swords, I am for you; in this I would be loth to prick my Finger. And where you say I wrong'd you, 'tis so far from my profession, that amongst my fears, to do wrong is the greatest: credit me we have been both abused, (not by our selves, for that I hold a spleen, no sin of malice, and may with man enough be best forgoten,) but by that willfull, scornful piece of hatred, that much forgetful Lady: for whose sake, if we should leave our reason, and run on upon our sense, like *Rams*, the little world of good men would laugh at us, and despise us, fixing upon our desperate memories the never-worn out names of Fools and Fencers. Sir 'tis not fear, but reason makes me tell you; in this I had rather help you Sir, than hurt you, and you shall find it, though you throw your self into as many dangers as she offers, though you redeem her lost name every day, and find her out new honours with your Sword, you shall but be her mirth as I have been.

Wel. I ask you mercy Sir, you have ta'ne my edge off: yet I would fain be even with this Lady.

Elder Lo. In which I'le be your helper: we are two, and they are two: two Sisters, rich alike, only the elder has the prouder Dowry: In troth I pity this disgrace in you, yet of mine own I am senceless: do but follow my Counsel, and I'le pawn my spirit, we'l overreach 'em yet; the means is this —

Enter Servant.

Ser. Sir there's a Gentlewoma[n] will needs speak with you, I cannot keep her out, she's entred Sir.

Elder Lo. It is the waiting woman, pray be not seen: sirrah hold her in discourse a while: hark in your ear, go and dispatch it quickly, when I come in, I'le tell you all the project.

Wel. I care not which I have. [*Exit* Welford.

Elder Lo. Away, 'tis done, she must not see you: now Lady *Guiniver* what news with you?

Enter Abigal.

Abig. Pray leave these frumps Sir, and receive this letter.

Elder Lo. From whom good vanity?

Abig. 'Tis from my Lady Sir: Alas good soul, she cries and takes on!

Elder Lo. Do's she so good Soul? wou'd she not have a Cawdle? do's she send you with your fine Oratory goody *Tully* to tye me to believe again? bring out the Cat-hounds, I'le make you take a tree Whore, then with my tiller bring down your *Gibship*, and then have you cast, and hung up i'th' Warren.

Abig. I am no beast Sir, would you knew it.

Elder Lo. Wou'd I did, for I am yet very doubtful; what will you say now?

Abig. Nothing not I.

Elder Lo. Art thou a woman, and say nothing?

Abig. Unless you'l hear me with more moderation, I can speak wise enough.

Elder Lo. And loud enough? will your Lady love me?

Abig. It seems so by her letter, and her lamentations; but you are such another man.

Elder Lo. Not such another as I was, Mumps; nor will not be: I'le read her fine Epistle: ha, ha, ha, is not thy Mistress mad?

Abig. For you she will be, 'tis a shame you should use a poor Gentlewoman so untowardly; she loves the ground you tread on; and you (hard heart) because she jested with you, mean to kill her; 'tis a fine conquest as they say.

Elder Lo. Hast thou so much moisture in the Whitleather hide yet, that thou canst cry? I wou'd have sworn thou hadst been touchwood five year since; nay let it rain, thy face chops for a shower like a dry Dunghil.

Abig. I'le not indure this Ribauldry; farewel i'th' Devils name; if my Lady die, I'le be sworn before a Jury, thou art the cause on't.

Elder Lo. Do Maukin do, deliver to your Lady from me this: I mean to see her, if I have no other business: which before I'le want to come to her, I mean to go seek birds nests: yet I may come too: but if I come, from this door till I see her, will I think how to rail vildly at her; how to vex her, and make her cry so much, that the Physician if she fall sick upon't, shall find the cause to be want of Urine, and she remediless dye in her Heresie: Farewell old Adage, I hope to see the Boys make Potguns on thee.

Abig. Th'art a vile man, God bless my issue from thee.

Elder Lo. Thou hast but one, and that's in thy left crupper, that makes thee hobble so; you must be ground i'th' breach like a Top, you'l ne're spin well else: Farewell Fytchock. [*Exeunt.*

Enter Lady *alone.*

Lady. Is it not strange that every womans will should track out new wayes to disturb her self? if I should call my reason to account, it cannot answer why I keep my self from mine own wish, and stop the man I love from his; and every hour repent again, yet still go on: I know 'tis like a man, that wants his natural sleep, and growing dull would gladly give the remnant of his life for two hours rest; yet through his frowardness, will rather choose to watch another man, drowsie as he, than take his own repose. All this I know: yet a strange peevishness and anger, not to have the power to do things unexpected, carries me away to mine own ruine: I had rather die sometimes than not disgrace in public him whom people think I love, and do't with oaths, and am in earnest then: O what are we! Men, you must answer this, that dare obey such things as we command. How now? what newes?

Enter Abigal.

Abi. Faith Madam none worth hearing.

Lady. Is he not come?

Abi. No truly.

Lady. Nor has he writ?

Abigal. Neither. I pray God you have not undone your self.

Lady. Why, but what saies he?

Abi. Faith he talks strangely.

Lady. How strangely?

Abi. First at your Letter he laught extremely.

Lady. What, in contempt?

Abi. He laught monstrous loud, as he would die, and when you wrote it I think you were in no such merry mood, to provoke him that way: and having done he cried Alas for her, and violently laught again.

Lady. Did he?

Abi. Yes, till I was angry.

Lady. Angry, why? why wert thou angry? he did doe but well, I did deserve it, he had been a fool, an unfit man for any one to love, had he not laught thus at me: you were angry, that show'd your folly; I shall love him more for that, than all that ere he did before: but said he nothing else?

Abi. Many uncertain things: he said though you had mockt him, because you were a woman, he could wish to do you so much favour as to see you: yet he said, he knew you rash, and was loth to offend you with the sight of one, whom now he was bound not to leave.

Lady. What one was that?

Abi. I know not, but truly I do fear there is a making up there: for I heard the servants, as I past by some, whisper such a thing: and as I came back through the hall, there were two or three Clarks writing great conveyances in hast, which they said were for their Mistris joynture.

Lady. 'Tis very like, and fit it should be so, for he does think, and reasonably think, that I should keep him with my idle tricks for ever ere he be married.

Abi. At last he said, it should go hard but he would see you for your satisfaction.

Lady. All we that are called Women, know as well as men, it were a far more noble thing to grace where we are grace't, and give respect there where we are respected: yet we practise a wilder course, and never bend our eyes on men with pleasure, till they find the way to give us a neglect: then we, too late, perceive the loss of what we might have had, and dote to death.

Enter Martha.

Mar. Sister, yonder's your Servant, with a Gentlewoman with him.

Lady. Where?

Mar. Close at the door.

Lady. Alas I am undone, I fear he is be[t]roth'd, What kind of woman is she?

Mar. A most ill favoured one, with her Masque on: And how her face should mend the rest I know not.

La. But yet her mind was of a milder stuff than mine was.

Enter Elder Loveless, *and* Welford *in Womans apparel.*

Lady. Now I see him, if my heart swell not again (away thou womans pride) so that I cannot speak a gentle word to him, let me not live.

Elder Lo. By your leave here.

Lady. How now, what new trick invites you hither? Ha'you a fine device again?

Elder Lo. Faith this is the finest device I have now: How dost thou sweet heart?

Wel. Why very well, so long as I may please You my dear Lover. I nor can, nor will Be ill when you are well, well when you are ill.

Elder Lo. O thy sweet temper! what would I have given, that Lady had been like thee: seest thou her? that face (my love) join'd with thy humble mind, had made a wench indeed.

Wel. Alas my love, what God hath done, I dare not think to mend. I use no paint, nor any drugs of Art, my hands and face will shew it.

La. Why what thing have you brought to shew us there? do you take mony for it?

Elder Lo. A Godlike thing, not to be bought for mony: 'tis my Mistris: in whom there is no passion, nor no scorn: what I will is for law; pray you salute her.

Lady. Salute her? by this good light, I would not kiss her for half my wealth.

Elder Lo. Why? why pray you? You shall see me do't afore you; look you.

Lady. Now fie upon thee, a beast would not have don't. I would not kiss thee of a month to gain a Kingdom.

Elder Lo. Marry you shall not be troubled.

Lady. Why was there ever such a *Meg* as this? Sure thou art mad.

Elder Lo. I was mad once, when I lov'd pictures; for what are shape and colours else, but pictures? in that tawnie hide there lies an endless mass of vertues, when all your red and white ones want it.

Lady. And this is she you are to marry, is't not?

Elder Lo. Yes indeed is't.

Lady. God give you joy.

Elder Lo. Amen.

Wel. I thank yo[u], as unknown for your good wish. The like to you when ever you shall wed.

Elder Lo. O gentle Spirit!

Lady. You thank me? I pray Keep your breath nearer you, I do not like it.

Wel. I would not willingly offend at all, Much less a Lady of your worthie parts.

Elder Lo. Sweet, Sweet!

La. I do not think this woman can by nature be thus, Thus ugly; sure she's some common Strumpet, Deform'd with exercise of sin?

Wel. O Sir believe not this, for Heaven so comfort me as I am free from foul pollution with any man; my honour ta'ne away, I am no woman.

Elder Lo. Arise my dearest Soul; I do not credit it. Alas, I fear her tender heart will break with this reproach; fie that you know no more civility to a weak Virgin. 'Tis no matter Sweet, let her say what she will, thou art not worse to me, and therefore not at all; be careless.

Wel. For all things else I would, but for mine honor; Me thinks.

Elder Lo. Alas, thine honour is not stain'd, Is this the business that you sent for me about?

Mar. Faith Sister you are much to blame, to use a woman, whatsoe're she be, thus; I'le salute her: You are welcome hither.

Wel. I humbly thank you.

Elder Lo. Milde yet as the Dove, for all these injuries. Come shall we goe, I love thee not so ill to keep thee here a jesting stock. Adue to the worlds end.

Lady. Why whither now?

Elder Lo. Nay you shall never know, because you shall not find me.

Lady. I pray let me speak with you.

Elder Lo. 'Tis very well: come.

Lady. I pray you let me speak with you.

Elder Lo. Yes for another mock.

Lady. By Heaven I have no mocks: good Sir a word.

Elder Lo. Though you deserve not so much at my hands, yet if you be in such earnest, I'le speak a word with you; but I beseech you be brief: for in good faith there's a Parson and a licence stay for us i'th' Church all this while: and you know 'tis night.

Lady. Sir, give me hearing patiently, and whatsoever I have heretofore spoke jestingly, forget: for as I hope for mercy any where, what I shall utter now is from my heart, and as I mean.

Elder Lo. Well, well, what do you mean?

Lady. Was not I once your Mistress, and you my Servant?

Elder Lo. O 'tis about the old matter.

Lady. Nay good Sir stay me out; I would but hear you excuse your self, why you should take this woman, and leave me.

Elder Lo. Prethee why not, deserves she not as much as you?

Lady. I think not, if you will look With an indifferency upon us both.

Elder Lo. Upon your faces, 'tis true: but if judiciously we shall cast our eyes upon your minds, you are a thousand women of her in worth: she cannot swound in jest, nor set her lover tasks, to shew her peevishness, and his affection, nor cross what he saies, though it be Canonical. She's a good plain wench, that will do as I will have her, and bring me lusty Boys to throw the Sledge, and lift at Pigs of Lead: and for a Wife, she's far beyond you: what can you do in a houshold to provide for your issue, but lye i' bed and get 'em? your business is to dress you, and at idle hours to eat; when she can do a thousand profitable things: she can do pretty well in the Pastry, and knows how Pullen should be cram'd, she cuts Cambrick at a thread, weaves Bone-lace, and quilts Balls; and what are you good for?

Lady. Admit it true, that she were far beyond me in all respects, does that give you a licence to forswear your self?

Elder Lo. Forswear my self, how?

Lady. Perhaps you have forgotten the innumerable oaths you have utter'd in disclaiming all for Wives but me: I'le not remember you: God give you joy.

Elder Lo. Nay but conceive me, the intent of oaths is ever understood: Admit I should protest to such a friend, to see him at his Lodging to morrow: Divines would never hold me perjur'd if I were struck blind, or he hid him where my diligent search could not find him: so there were no cross act of mine own in't. Can it be imagined I mean to force you to Marriage, and to have you whether you will or no?

Lady. Alas you need not. I make already tender of my self, and then you are forsworn.

Elder Lo. Some sin I see indeed must necessarily fall upon me, as whosoever deals with Women shall never utterly avoid it: yet I would chuse the least ill; which is to forsake you, that have done me all the abuses of a malignant Woman, contemn'd my service, and would have held me prating about Marriage, till I had been past getting of Children: then her that hath forsaken her Family, and put her tender body in my hand, upon my word —

Lady. Which of us swore you first to?

Elder Lo. Why to you.

Lady. Which oath is to be kept then?

Elder Lo. I prethee do not urge my sins unto me, Without I could amend 'em.

Lady. Why you may by wedding me.

Elder Lo. How will that satisfie my word to her?

Lady. 'Tis not to be kept, and needs no satisfaction, 'Tis an error fit for repentance only.

Elder Lo. Shall I live to wrong that tender hearted Virgin so? It may not be.

Lady. Why may it not be?

Elder Lo. I swear I would rather marry thee than her: but yet mine honesty?

Lady. What honesty? 'Tis more preserv'd this way: Come, by this light, servant, thou shalt, I'le kiss thee on't.

Elder Lo. This kiss indeed is sweet, pray God no sin lie under it.

Lady. There is no sin at all, try but another.

Wel. O my heart!

Mar. Help Sister, this Lady swounds.

Elder Lo. How do you?

Wel. Why very well, if you be so.

Elder Lo. Since a quiet mind lives not in any Woman, I shall do a most ungodly thing. Hear me one word more, which by all my hopes I will not alter, I did make an oath when you delai'd me so, that this very night I would be married. Now if you will go without delay, suddenly, as late as it is, with your own Minister to your own Chapel, I'le wed you and to bed.

Lady. A match dear servant.

Elder Lo. For if you should forsake me now, I care not, she would not though for all her injuries, such is her spirit. If I be not ashamed to kiss her now I part, may I not live.

Wel. I see you go, as slily as you think to steal away: yet I will pray for you; all blessings of the world light on you two, that you may live to be an aged pair. All curses on me if I do not speak what I do wish indeed.

Elder Lo. If I can speak to purpose to her, I am a villain.

Lady. Servant away.

Mar. Sister, will you Marry that inconstant man? think you he will not cast you off to morrow, to wrong a Lady thus, lookt she like dirt, 'twas basely done. May you ne're prosper with him.

Wel. Now God forbid. Alas I was unworthy, so I told him.

Mar. That was your modesty, too good for him. I would not see your wedding for a world.

Lady. Chuse chuse, come *Younglove.*

[*Exit* La. Elder Lo. *and* Young.

Mar. Dry up your eyes forsooth, you shall not think we are all such uncivil beasts as these. Would I knew how to give you a revenge.

Wel. So would not I: No let me suffer truly, that I desire.

Mar. Pray walk in with me, 'tis very late, and you shall stay all night: your bed shall be no worse than mine; I wish I could but do you right.

Wel. My humble thanks: God grant I may but live to quit your love. [*Exeunt.*

Enter Young Loveless *and* Savil.

Young Lo. Did your Master send for me *Savil*?

Sav. Yes, he did send for your worship Sir.

Young Lo. Do you know the business?

Sav. Alas Sir, I know nothing, nor am imployed beyond my hours of eating. My dancing days are done Sir.

Young Lo. What art thou now then?

Sav. If you consider me in little, I am with your worships reverence Sir, a Rascal: one that upon the next anger of your Brother, must raise a sconce by the high way, and sell switches; my wife is learning now Sir, to weave inkle.

Young Lo. What dost thou mean to do with thy Children *Savil*?

Sav. My eldest boy is half a Rogue already, he was born bursten, and your worship knows, that is a pretty step to mens compassions. My youngest boy I purpose Sir to bind for ten years to a G[ao]ler, to draw under him, that he may shew us mercy in his function.

Young Lo. Your family is quartered with discretion: you are resolved to Cant then: where *Savil* shall your scene lie?

Sav. Beggers must be no chusers. In every place (I take it) but the stocks.

Young Lo. This is your drinking, and your whoring *Savil*, I told you of it, but your heart was hardened.

Sav. 'Tis true, you were the first that told me of it I do remember yet in tears, you told me you would have Whores, and in that passion Sir, you broke out thus; Thou miserable man, repent, and brew three Strikes more in a Hogshead. 'Tis noon e're we be drunk now, and the time can tarry for no man.

Young Lo. Y'are grown a bitter Gentleman. I see misery can clear your head better than Mustard, I'le be a sutor for your Keys again Sir.

Sav. Will you but be so gracious to me Sir? I shall be bound.

Young Lo. You shall Sir To your bunch again, or I'le miss foully.

Enter Morecraft.

Mor. Save you Gentleman, save you.

Young Lo. Now Polecat, what young Rabets nest have you to draw?

Mor. Come, prethee be familiar Knight.

Young Lo. Away Fox, I'le send for Terriers for you.

Mor. Thou art wide yet: I'le keep thee companie.

Young Lo. I am about some business; Indentures, If ye follow me I'le beat you: take heed, A[s] I live I'le cancel your Coxcomb.

Mor. Thou art cozen'd now, I am no usurer: What poor fellow's this?

Savil. I am poor indeed Sir.

Mor. Give him mony Knight.

Young Lo. Do you begin the offering.

Mor. There poor fellow, here's an Angel for thee.

Young Lo. Art thou in earnest *Morecraft*?

Mor. Yes faith Knight, I'le follow thy example: thou hadst land and thousands, thou spendst, and flungst away, and yet it flows in double: I purchased, wrung, and wierdraw'd, for my wealth, lost, and was cozen'd: for which I make a vow, to trie all the waies above ground, but I'le find a constant means to riches without curses.

Young Lo. I am glad of your conversion Master *Morecraft*: Y'are in a fair course, pray pursue it still.

Mor. Come, we are all gallants now, I'le keep thee company; Here honest fellow, for this Gentlemans sake, there's two Angels more for thee.

Savil. God quite you Sir, and keep you long in this mind.

Young Lo. Wilt thou persevere?

Mor. Till I have a penny. I have brave cloathes a making, and two horses; canst thou not help me to a match Knight, I'le lay a thousand pound upon my crop-ear.

Yo. Lo. Foot, this is stranger than an *Africk* monster, There will be no more talk of the *Cleve* wars Whilst this lasts, come, I'le put thee into blood.

Sav. Would all his damn'd tribe were as tender hearted. I beseech you let this Gentleman join with you in the recovery of my Keyes; I like his good beginning Sir, the whilst I'le pray for both your worships.

Young Lo. He shall Sir.

Mor. Shall we goe noble Knight? I would fain be acquainted.

Young Lo. I'le be your Servant Sir. [*Exeunt.*

Enter Elder Loveless, *and* Lady.

Elder Lo. Faith my sweet Lady, I have caught you now, maugre your subtilties, and fine devices, be coy again now.

Lady. Prethee sweet-heart tell true.

Elder Lo. By this light, by all the pleasures I have had this night, by your lost maidenhead, you are cozened meerly. I have cast beyond your wit. That Gentleman is your retainer *Welford*.

Lady. It cannot be so.

Elder Lo. Your Sister has found it so, or I mistake, mark how she blushes when you see her next. Ha, ha, ha, I shall not travel now, ha, ha, ha.

Lady. Prethee sweet heart be quiet, thou hast angred me at heart.

Elder Lo. I'le please you soon again.

La. Welford?

Elder Lo. I *Welford*, hee's a young handsome fellow, well bred and landed, your Sister can instruct you in his good parts, better than I by this time.

Lady. Uds foot am I fetcht over thus?

Elder Lo. Yes i'faith. And over shall be fetcht again, never fear it.

Lady. I must be patient, though it torture me: You have got the Sun Sir.

Elder Lo. And the Moon too, in which I'le be the man.

Lady. But had I known this, had I but surmiz'd it, you should have hunted three trains more, before you had come to th' course, you should have hankt o'th' bridle, Sir, i'faith.

El. Lo. I knew it, and min'd with you, and so blew you up. Now you may see the Gentlewoman: stand close.

Enter Welford, *and* Martha.

Mar. For Gods sake Sir, be private in this business, You have un-done me else. O God, what have I done?

Wel. No harm I warrant thee.

Mar. How shall I look upon my friends again? With what face?

Wel. Why e'ne with that: 'tis a good one, thou canst not find a bet-ter: look upon all the faces thou shall see there, and you shall find 'em smooth still, fair still, sweet still, and to your thinking honest; those have done as much as you have yet, or dare doe Mistris, and yet they keep no stir.

Mar. Good Sir goe in, and put your womans cloaths on: If you be seen thus, I am lost for ever.

Wel. I'le watch you for that Mistris: I am no fool, here will I tarry till the house be up and witness with me.

Mar. Good dear friend goe in.

Wel. To bed again if you please, else I am fixt here till there be no-tice taken what I am, and what I have done: if you could juggle me into my woman-hood again, and so cog me out of your company, all this would be forsworn, and I again an *asinego*, as your Sister left me. No, I'le have it known and publisht; then if you'le be a whore, forsake me and be asham'd: and when you can hold no longer, mar-ry some cast *Cleve Captain,* and sell Bottle-ale.

Mar. I dare not stay Sir, use me modestly, I am your wife.

Wel. Goe in, I'le make up all.

Elder Lo. I'le be a witness of your naked truth Sir: this is the Gent-lewoman, prethee look upon him, that is he that made me break my faith sweet: but thank your Sister, she hath soder'd it.

Lady. What a dull ass was I, I could not see this wencher from a wench: twenty to one, if I had been but tender like my Sister, he had served me such a slippery trick too.

Wel. Twenty to one I had.

Elder Lo. I would have watcht you Sir, by your good patience, for ferreting in my ground.

Lady. You have been with my Sister.

Wel. Yes to bring.

Elder Lo. An heir into the world he means.

Lady. There is no chafing now.

Wel. I have had my part on't: I have been chaft this three hours, that's the least, I am reasonable cool now.

Lady. Cannot you fare well, but you must cry roast-meat?

Wel. He that fares well, and will not bless the founders, is either surfeited, or ill taught, Lady, for mine own part, I have found so sweet a diet, I can commend it, though I cannot spare it.

Elder Lo. How like you this dish, *Welford*, I made a supper on't, and fed so heartily, I could not sleep.

Lady. By this light, had I but scented out your [train], ye had slept with a bare pillow in your arms and kist that, or else the bed-post, for any wife ye had got this twelve-month yet: I would have vext you more than a try'd post-horse; and been longer bearing, than ever after-game at *Irish* was. Lord, that I were unmarried again.

Elder Lo. Lady I would not undertake ye, were you again a *Haggard*, for the best cast of four Ladys i'th' Kingdom: you were ever tickle-footed, and would not truss round.

Wel. Is she fast?

Elder Lo. She was all night lockt here boy.

Wel. Then you may lure her without fear of losing: take off her Cranes. You have a delicate Gentlewoman to your Sister: Lord what a prettie furie she was in, when she perceived I was a man: but I thank God I satisfied her scruple, without the Parson o'th' town.

Elder Lo. What did ye?

Wel. Madam, can you tell what we did?

Elder Lo. She has a shrewd guess at it I see it by her.

Lady. Well you may mock us: but my large Gentlewoman, my *Mary Ambre*, had I but seen into you, you should have had another bed-fellow, fitter a great deal for your itch.

Wel. I thank you Lady, me thought it was well, You are so curious.

Enter Young Loveless, *his* Lady, Morecraft, Savil, *and two Serving-men.*

El. Lo. Get on your doublet, here comes my Brother.

Yo. Lo. Good morrow Brother, and all good to your Lady.

Mor. God save you and good morrow to you all.

El. Lo. Good morrow. Here's a poor brother of yours.

Lady. Fie how this shames me.

Mor. Prethee good fellow help me to a cup of beer.

Ser. I will Sir.

Yo. Lo. Brother what makes you here? will this Lady do? Will she? is she not nettl'd still?

Elder Lo. No I have cur'd her. Mr. *Welford*, pray know this Gentleman is my Brother.

Wel. Sir I shall long to love him.

Yo. Lo. I shall not be your debter Sir. But how is't with you?

Elder Lo. As well as may be man: I am married: your new acquaintance hath her Sister, and all's well.

Yo. Lo. I am glad on't. Now my prettie Lady Sister, How do you find my Brother?

Lady. Almost as wild as you are.

Yo. Lo. He will make the better husband: you have tried him?

Lady. Against my will Sir.

Yo. Lo. Hee'l make your will amends soon, do not doubt it. But Sir I must intreat you to be better known To this converted *Jew* here.

Ser. Here's Beer for you Sir.

Mor. And here's for you an Angel: Pray buy no Land, 'twill never prosper Sir.

Elder Lo. How's this?

Yo. Lo. Bless you, and then I'le tell: He's turn'd Gallant.

Elder Lo. Gallant?

Yo. Lo. I Gallant, and is now called, *Cutting Morecraft*: The reason I'le inform you at more leisure.

Wel. O good Sir let me know him presently.

Young Lo. You shall hug one another.

Mor. Sir I must keep you company.

Elder Lo. And reason.

Young Lo. Cutting *Morecraft* faces about, I must present another.

Mor. As many as you will Sir, I am for 'em.

Wel. Sir I shall do you service.

Mor. I shall look for't in good faith Sir.

Elder Lo. Prethee good sweet heart kiss him.

Lady. Who, that fellow?

Savil. Sir will it please you to remember me: my keys good Sir.

Young Lo. I'le doe it presently.

El. Lo. Come thou shalt kiss him for our sport sake.

La. Let him come on then; and do you hear, do not instruct me in these tricks, for you may repent it.

El. Lo. That at my peril. Lusty Mr. *Morecraft*, Here is a Lady would salute you.

Mor. She shall not lose her longing Sir: what is she?

Elder Lo. My wife Sir.

Mor. She must be then my Mistres.

Lady. Must I Sir?

Elder Lo. O yes, you must.

Mor. And you must take this ring, a poor pawn Of some fiftie pound.

El Lo. Take it by any means, 'tis lawfull prize.

Lady. Sir I shall call you servant.

Mor. I shall be proud on't: what fellow's that?

Young Lo. My Ladies Coachman.

Mor. There's something, (my friend) for you to buy whips, And for you Sir, and you Sir.

Elder Lo. Under a miracle this is the strangest I ever heard of.

Mor. What, shall we play, or drink? what shall we doe? Who will hunt with me for a hundred pounds?

Wel. Stranger and Stranger! Sir you shall find sport after a day or two.

Young Lo. Sir I have a sute unto you Concerning your old servant *Savil.*

Elder Lo. O, for his keys, I know it.

Savil. Now Sir, strike in.

Mor. Sir I must have you grant me.

Elder Lo. 'Tis done Sir, take your keys again:
But hark you *Savil*, leave off the motions
Of the flesh, and be honest, or else you shall graze again:
I'le try you once more.

Savil. If ever I be taken drunk, or whoring, Take off the biggest key i'th' bunch, and open My head with it Sir: I humbly thank your worships.

Elder Lo. Nay then I see we must keep holiday. *Enter* Roger, *and* Abigal. Here's the last couple in hell.

Roger. Joy be among you all.

Lady. Why how now Sir, what is the meaning of this emblem?

Roger. Marriage an't like your worship.

Lady. Are you married?

Roger. As well as the next Priest could doe it, Madam.

Elder Lo. I think the sign's in *Gemini*, here's such coupling.

Wel. Sir *Roger*, what will you take to lie from your sweet-heart to night?

Roger. Not the best benefice in your worships gift Sir.

Wel. A whorson, how he swells.

Young Lo. How many times to night Sir *Roger*?

Roger. Sir you grow scurrilous: What I shall do, I shall do: I shall not need your help.

Young Lo. For horse flesh *Roger*.

Elder Lo. Come prethee be not angry, 'tis a day Given wholly to our mirth.

Lady. It shall be so Sir: Sir *Roger* and his Bride, We shall intreat to be at our charge.

El. Lo. Welford get you to the Church: by this light, You shall not lie with her again, till y'are married.

Wel. I am gone.

Mor. To every Bride I dedicate this day Six healths a piece, and it shall goe hard, But every one a Jewell: Come be mad boys.

El. Lo. Th'art in a good beginning: come who leads? Sir *Roger*, you shall have the *Van*: lead the way: Would every dogged wench had such a day. [*Exeunt.*

(A) The | Scornful | Ladie. | A Comedie. | As it was Acted (with great

applause) by the children of Her Majesties | Revels in the Blacke |
Fryers.
Written by | Fra. Beaumont and Jo. Fletcher, Gent. | London |
Printed for
Myles Partrich, and are to be sold | at his Shop at the George neere
St
Dunstans | Church in Fleet-streete. 1616.

(B) The | Scorneful | Ladie. | A Comedie. | As it was now lately
Acted (with | great applause) by the Kings | Majesties servants, at
the | Blacke Fryers. | Written by | Fra. Beaumont, and Jo. Fletcher,
| Gentlemen. | London, | Printed for M.P. and are to be sold by |
Thomas Jones, at the blacke Raven, in | the Strand. 1625.

(C) The | Scornefull | Ladie. | A Comedie. | As it was now lately
Acted (with great | applause) by the Kings Majesties Servants, | at
the Blacke-Fryers. | Written | By Fran: Beaumont, and Jo: Fletcher,
| Gentlemen. | The third Edition. | London. | Printed by B.A. and
T.F. for T. Jones, and are to be sold at his | Shop in St. Dunstans
Church-yard in Fleet-street. | 1630.

(D) The | Scornfull | Ladie. | A Comedy. | As it was now lately
Acted (with great | applause) by the Kings Majesties Servants, | at
the Blacke-Fryers. | Written by Francis Beaymont, and John Flet-
cher, Gentlemen. | The fourth Edition. | London, | Printed by A.M.
1635.

(E) The | Scornfull | Lady. | A Comedy. | As it was now lately
Acted (with great | applause) by the Kings Majesties Servants, [at
the Blacke-Fryers. | Written by Francis Beaumont, and John Flet-
cher. Gentlemen. | The fift Edition. | London, | Printed by M.P. for
Robert Wilson, and are to be sold at | his shop in Holborne at
Grayes-Inne Gate. | 1639.

(F) The | Scornfull | Lady. | A Comedy. | As it was Acted (with
great
applause) by | the late Kings Majesties Servants, | at the Black-
Fryers.
| Written by Francis Beaumont, and John Fletcher. Gentlemen. |
The sixt
Edition, Corrected and | amended. | London: | Printed for

Humphrey
Moseley, and are to be sold at his Shop | at the Princes Armes in St.
Pauls Church-yard. 1651.
(The British Museum copy lacks the printer's device on the title-
page,
possessed by other copies seen; it varies also slightly in spelling etc.)

(G) The | Scornful | Lady: | A | Comedy. | As it is now Acted at
the |
Theater Royal, | by | His Majesties Servants.
| Written by Francis Beaumont and John Fletcher Gent. | The Se-
venth
Edition. | London: | Printed by A. Maxwell and R. Roberts, for
D.N. and
T.C. and are | to be sold by Simon Neale, at the Three Pidgeons in |
Bedford-street in Covent-Garden, 1677.

p. 231,
l. 5. A omits list of Persons Represented in the Play.
    B—E print the list on the back of the title-page, under the
        heading 'The Actors are these.'
    In F and G the same list is printed on a separate page following
        the title-page.
    G] The Names of the Actors.
l. 8. B and C] the eldest. D—G] the elder.

    p. 232, l. 1. A] a Userer. l. 4. A] Savill make the boate stay. B *prints*
'*Savil*. Make the boat stay,' as if the rest of the speech were spoken
by Savil. C—G for '*Savil*' print '*Yo. Lo.*,' thus giving the words to
Young Loveless. l. 9. E and G] at home marry. l. 10. A—E and G]
your countrey. F] your own country. A and B] then to travell for
diseases, and returne following the Court in a nightcap, and die
without issue. l. 15. Here and throughout the scene for 'Younglove'
D—G] Abigall. l. 16. A—C] Mistres. D] Mistrisse. E—G] Mistris. l.
22. A and B] for me. l. 33. E—G *omit*] Exit.

p. 233, l. 2. G] acted Loves. l. 3. A, B and E−G] murtherers. l. 6. A and B] that shall be. l. 12. A−G] woman. l. 25. A−G *omit*] and. l. 31. F] out there. l. 35. D−G for *Younglove*] Abigall.

p. 234, l. 5. F] time of place. l. 16. E−G *omit*] Yes. l. 19. E−G] that can. l. 27. F] deadfull. l. 37. G] and put. l. 39. A and B] with you for laughter.

p. 235, l. 10. A and B] and so you satisfied. l. 17. B] doeth. l. 28. A] Hipochrists. E and F] Hipocrasse. G] Hippocrass. l. 34. A and B] his yeere. l. 31. G] said she.

p. 236, l. 9. B] doeth. D and E] with you. l. 17. G *omits one*] that. l. 19. G] I'le live.

p. 237, l. 1. A and B] with three guards. l. 4. D] wesse. E−G] wisse. l. 10. D−G] Abigall. l. 14. E−G] happily. l. 21. A−E] may call. l. 25. A−G] as on others. A−G *omit*] that. l. 27. A−G] A my credit. l. 30. A and B] beginnings. l. 31. G] maid. l. 32. E and G] bed. l. 33. D−G] doe you not. l. 35. D−G] Abigall.

p. 238, l. 2. A and B] rid hard. l. 25. A] other woemen the households of. B−G] of the households. G] of as good. l. 28. F and G] tho not so coy. D−G] Abigall. l. 36. A−G] God.

p. 239, l. 7. G] Call'd. l. 17. A] your names. l. 32. A] the weomen. l. 33. A and B] an needlesse. E−G *omit*] a. F] her comes. G *and sometimes* F] here comes.

p. 240, l. 4. E−G *omit*] of. F and G] I do inculcate Divine Homilies. l. 13. G] man neglect. l. 16. A and B] I pray ye. A−G] and whilst. l. 19. B] your Lay. l. 20. C−F] ingenuous. l. 23. A] I shall beate. l. 25. A−E] forget one, who. F and G] forget then who. l. 34. A and B] how Hoppes goe.

p. 241, l. 6 A−G] to keep. l. 14. F and G] like a Gentlemen. l. 15. F *omits*] me. l. 23. D−G] Yet, that. l. 25. A−E *omit*] of. F and G] Ile here no more, this is. l. 30. A−E and G] comes. l. 39. A] Gent.

p. 242, l. 6. A−G *omit*] etc. l. 7. B−G] help all. l. 22. A and B] warre, that cries. l. 27. G] has knockt. l. 32. D−G *omit*] even. A−G] a conscience. l. 34. A−E *omit*] he.

p. 243, l. 6. E−G] pound. l. 11. A and B] We will have nobody talke wisely neither. F] Will you not. l. 17. A−C] ath Coram. l. 25. F and G *omit*] that. l. 27. F and G] sir, to expound it. l. 28. 2nd Folio *misprints*] iuterpretation. l. 37. A and B *omit*] Sir. l. 40. F *omits*] keep.

p. 244, l. 1. F and G *add after* part] Savil. l. 6. D−G *add*] Finis Actus Primus. F and G *add*] Omnes. O brave Loveless! (F=Lovelace) Exeunt omnes. l. 12. F and G *omit*] Lady. l. 13. F and G] that complaint. l. 28. F and G] it loveth. l. 34. A] premised.

p. 245, l. 11. D−G] reprov'd him. l. 22. F and G] hath made. l. 23. A and B *misprint*] Maria. l. 25. F and G] with a. l. 27. A and B] He's fast. l. 39. F and G *omit*] Sir.

p. 246, l. 4. A, B and G] Gentlewoman. l. 23. G *omits*] indeed. l. 26. F and G] smile hath. l. 28. A−E and G] cropping off. l. 34. E and G] meditations. l. 36. F and G] and experience the. E−G] collection. l. 39. F and G] thus to.

p. 248, ll. 3 and 4. G] and fornication. l. 24. A and G] set.

p. 249, l. 10. A−C, E−G] appeares. l. 11. A] drown. l. 12. G] Sir Aeneas. l. 34. A and B] Gentlewoman.

p. 250, l. 15. A−G] a Gods name.

p. 251, l. 11. A and B *add*] Drinke to my friend Captaine. l. 14. A, B, F and G *add at end*] Sir. l. 15. A−G] cursie. F] a tittle. l. 16. G] would strive, Sir. F] I will strive, Sir. l. 22. Second Folio *misprints*] Youn. l. 24. A] to feede more fishes. l. 30. F and G] pray you let. l. 34. A] a ful rouse. ll. 36 and 37. D and F] I bear. l. 39. A−G] a your knees.

p. 252, l. 12. A] finde. l. 32. F and G *for* Capt. (character) *read* Sav. *and add* 'Let's in and drink and give' etc.

p. 253, l. 5. F and G] be you your. l. 27. D−F] love chamber. G] dares. l. 34. A−C] will stoop. l. 35. A] feede ill. l. 36. A−G] which for I was his wife and gave way to. l. 39. F] in patience of.

p. 254, l. 1. D and E] gossip too. l. 3. E and F] from whence. l. 9. F *misprints*] crown'd at. l. 21. E−G] have the money. l. 23. F and G] provided my wise. l. 26. F] Here's here. ll. 30 and 31. F and G] for thine. l. 32. F *omits*] well.

p. 255, l. 1. A] the faith. l. 11. D−G] mony fit for. l. 13. A−D, F and G] afore. l. 14. G *omits*] all. ll. 18 and 19. D−G] turne up. l. 20.

G] Ship. l. 22. G] poor man. l. 26. D, F and G] against the. l. 28. A—
G] thy staffe of office there, thy pen and Ink-horne. Noble boy. l. 29.
A] sed. ll. 30 and 31. A—G] thy seat. l. 34. F and G] men immortal. l.
37. A] that shall. l. 40. A] What meane they Captaine.

p. 256, l. 8. F and G] pounds. l. 9. F and G] by this hand. l. 13. F
and G] There is six Angels in earnest. l. 17. A] all in. l. 25. F and G
omit] so be it. l. 35. A and B] at charge. l. 40. A—G *add*] Finis Actus
Secundi.

p. 257, l. 2. A *omits*] and drops her glove. l. 3. A—C] tels. l. 8. A, B
and D—G] Lenvoy. l. 16. F and G] No, Sir.

p. 258, l. 10. D, E and G] come here to speak with. l. 18. F and G] I
say I. l. 26. A *misprints*] ralkt. F and G] with the. l. 29. F and G] Troth
guess. l. 33. F] Gentlewomen. l. 36. A and B] But one, I am. C] or
Woman.

p. 259, l. 1. A] shall not you. l. 16. A—C and E—G] no such. l. 19.
A—C and E—G] tender Sir, whose gentle bloud. l. 29. A *omits*] be. l.
31. A and G] as he. l. 34. A *omits*] They draw. l. 36. F and G *omit*]
Jesus.

p. 260, l. 4. A and B *omit*] Why. l. 11. F] but none so. l. 26. A]wilde
B, C and E—G] vild. l. 31. F and G] sword. l. 33. B and G] a hazard.

p. 261, l. 1. A and B] which is prone inough. C—G] are prone. l. 5.
A] anger lost. l. 10. F and G] least share in. l. 25. D, F and G] are you.
l. 33. A and B] self from such temptations. G] self from temptations.
l. 34. A—D, F and G] Pray leape. G] the matter. C] whether would. l.
38. A—C, E and G] should.

p. 262, l. 6. F and G *omit*] a. l. 11. A—C] see. l. 12. E] Of any. l. 20. F
and G] his ruin. l. 27. C *omits*] him. E—G] with these. l. 37. E—G]
leave them to others. l. 40. C] works a mine.

p. 263, l. 13. A] certaine. l. 18. E—G] spoken. l. 19. F] ask you. l. 20.
E—G] forward. l. 32. G] hard-hearted. l. 35. F and G] me to do.

p. 264, l. 4. E—G] could redeem. l. 10. D, F and G] This. l. 24. A]
you have so. l. 27. E and G] By this light.

p. 265, l. 10. F] by your troth. l. 11. A] could. l. 15. C] cold meats. l.
23. F and G] we would. l. 27. F and G] that thou art here. l. 29. F and

G] use thee. l. 33. A and B] offending. l. 34. F and G] Thou art nothing … for love's sake.

p. 266, l. 3. G *omits*] I hope. l. 13. F and G] thy face. l. 14. A−G *omit*] for. ll. 21 and 22. F and G] companion. l. 25. A] amable. l. 38. G *adds at end*] I hope.

p. 267, l. 4. A, B and D−F] Don Diego, Ile. l. 11. A, C and E] saies. l. 15. E−G] you may. l. 20. E] wine here. F and G *add before* All] Mr. Morecraft. l. 21. A−G] Sir. *Savill?* l. 31. G] and yet they. l. 33. F *omits*] pray. l. 36. A−C and E−G] God a gold. 2nd Folio *misprints*] expouud.

p. 268, l. 3. A] not you. l. 7. A and B] is much is much. l. 18. G] in tenements of. l. 22. F and G] I shall not dare to. l. 23. A] By blithe. l. 33. A and B] of satten. l. 37. A−G] necessary. D−G] and consuming.

p. 269, l. 10. 2nd Folio *misprints*] nor. l. 16. A−G] a' my knowledge. l. 20. F and G] the. F] Morall. l. 27. B and D−G] worst on's. l. 31. A] your complement. l. 34. F and G] paid back again.

p. 270, l. 4. F and G] we have liv'd. ll. 4 and 5. F and G] be the hour that. l. 14. A *misprints*] Yo. Lo. l. 15. F and G] A thirsty. l. 17. F *omits*] Sir. l. 20. A] raile. l. 24. D−G] to'th.

p. 271, l. 1. A] hee's your. l. 4. A−G] fall. l. 19. A−G] who you left me too. l. 20. F *omits*] for. l. 23. F and G] be leaping in. l. 24. E−G] nights. l. 25. F *omits*] my. l. 27. E] thirtie. l. 34. B] you fellow. l. 37. A−G] Cresses sir to coole. l. 39. A−C] fornications.

p. 272, l. 3. E−G] get no. l. 4. A−G *add*] Finis Actus tertii. l. 6. A−G] solus. l. 8. A] thee to? to what scurvy Fortune. l. 9. E] of Noblemen. l. 15. B and E−G] profit. 2nd Folio *misprints*] Eccle. l. 16. F] eats out youth. l. 22. 2nd Folio *misprints*] abolishth, is. l. 25. D and E] in his. l. 33. A] neglectingly. l. 34. A] broke.

p. 273, l. 9. F and G] abused like me. A−F] Dalida. l. 11. F and G] you may dilate. l. 27. F and G] could not expound. l. 28. A] and then at prayers once (out of the stinking stir you put me in). l. 29. A] mine owne royall [F and G *also add* royal] issue. l. 34. D and E] for you. l. 35 B] and thus. l. 36. A, F and G] contrition, as a Father saith.

l. 39. A—G] Comfets. l. 40. A, F and G] then a long chapter with a pedigree.

p. 274, l. 3. A] lovely. l. 4. F and G] when due time. l. 8. F and G] but have. l. 14. A—E] cunny. l. 17. A *omits*] in. F and G] the hanging. l. 19. A, F and G] more with the great Booke of Martyrs. l. 23. F and G *add after* beloved] Abigail. l. 31. E—G] chop up.

p. 275, l. 3. A and B] wise Sir. l. 7. A, B, F and G] make. l. 14. F and G] thank Heaven. l. 19. E—G *omit*] Lord. l. 22. A and B] some sow. l. 23. F and G] brought forth. l. 26. F and G] will not. l. 29. E] a cleere. E—G] would take. l. 39. A] and yet would.

p. 276, l. 3. A—F] errant. l. 5. A—F] pray be. l. 9. A] the gods (B=God) knowes. C] God the knowes. F and G] Heaven knows. l. 15. 2nd Folio *misprints*] Lo. l. 18. A *omits*] so. l. 19. A—C *omit*] for. l. 38. E—G] that has.

p. 277, l. 1. A and B] turne in to. l. 4. A *omits*] pray. l. 13. G] have you. l. 14. G] light, as spirited. l. 21. G] sheeps. l. 22. G] with two. l. 23. F and G *add at end*] I can. l. 33. F and G] your use of. l. 37. A, B, D, F and G] now then.

p. 278, l. 7. A—G] Rosasolis. l. 16. G] in presuming thus. l. 19. F—G] to any end. l. 23. D, E and G] heap affliction. B—D, F and G] on me. l. 28. F and G *add*] ha. l. 33. F and G *for a read*] ha'. l. 37. E—G *omit*] Sir.

p. 279, l. 1. G] no so. l. 2. A] know. l. 6. F *omits*] that. ll. 6—8. D and E *omit*] at you ...not laugh *and runs on the remainder of* Lady's *speech as part of* Mar.'s. F and G *omit*] Sir ...not laugh. l. 7. A—C *omit one*] 'ha.' l. 15. A and B] for it then. l. 20. E—G] And you may. l. 28. G] crack. l. 36. A—C] fit ath. l. 38. B] will you cure.

p. 280, l. 5. A and C] Let him alone, 'is crackt. l. 6. D—G] he's a beastly. A and B] to loose. l. 7. A—G] is a. ll. 9 and 10. G] foh (soh F) she stinks. ll. 19 and 20. F and G] ye have ...hate ye. l. 23. A and B] in intercession. D—G] make intercession. l. 25. A] not all. l. 26. F and G] and will. l. 32. A and B] safer dote. l. 33. F] disease.

p. 281, l. 8. A—C] I hope 'is not. l. 16. A] There is. l. 28. A] Carrire. D—G] carriage. l. 29. A—C, F and G] now I. l. 30. A—G] a horse back. l. 31. A—C and E—G] to looke to.

p. 282, l. 3. A—C] 'is fleet. l. 10. 2nd Folio *misprints*] sweed. l. 11. F] not your. A—E] Reasens. F and G] your rotten Reasons. l. 13. F and G] civil and feed. l. 16. A—G] pounds. l. 18. A, F and G] defend.

p. 283, l. 2. F and G] Ordinaries do eat. l. 3. F and G] to a play. l. 6. E] Bootmaker. F and G] to a bear-baiting. l. 13. A, C—G] aire. l. 15. A] as little. l. 18. E] if they may. ll. 22 and 23. F and G] ask me. l. 23. A and B] a modesty. l. 24. A—F] Wardrope. l. 28. E—G] to dogs. l. 36 E] cheate. A—G] *add*] Finis Actus Quarti.

p. 284, l. 27. F and G] the Gentleman. l. 31. A and B] house Sir.

p. 285, l. 5. B] for your. l. 10. A—D] be lest. E—G] be left. l. 15. E] never-worme. l. 25. F and G] the elder hath. l. 31. 2nd Folio *misprints*] Gentlewomau.

p. 286, l. 7. G] goodly. l. 8. A and D] beliefe. l. 10. E—G] you cas'd. l. 29. A—G] in thy. l. 30. G *omits*] I. l. 31. F] years.

p. 287, l. 1. F and G] vilely. l. 3. A and D—G] shall want uryne to finde the cause by: and she. B and C] shall want uryne finde the cause be. l. 14. A and B] I stoppe.

p. 288, l. 7. E *omits*] did. F and G] he does. l. 25. A and B *omit*] be. l. 34. F and G] till death.

p. 289, l. 1. 2nd Folio *misprints*] berroth'd. E and G *add at beginning*] Ah. l. 5. A and B] mind is. l. 6. G] womens. l. 22. F] not any. l. 26. F and G *omit*] Godlike. l. 27. A and B] passions. l. 28. F and G] is her law. l. 39. D—G] and colour.

p. 290, l. 7. 2nd Folio *misprints*] yon. l. 7. F and G] you, though unknown. l. 18. F and G] Heaven to comfort. l. 34. A and B] Milde still as. l. 37. B] ends. l. 40. F and G] never find.

p. 291, l. 7. A and B] I will. l. 12. G] spoken. l. 25. A—F] judicially. l. 27. G] off her. A—C] sound. G] her Love. F] lovers. l. 33. A, B and E—G] a bed. l. 37. D] at a third. F and G *add after* Balls] admirably.

p. 292, l. 2. A, F and G] forgot. ll. 4 and 5. F and G *omit*] I'll not … you joy. l. 9. G] there was. l. 10. A, B, F and G] meant. G *omits*] you. l. 19. G] rather then. l. 20. A, B and D—F] forsooke. l. 34. A, E and G] I had rather.

p. 293, l. 4. D−G *add after* so] a most ungodly thing. ll. 5 and 6. D−G *omit*] Since a … ungodly thing. l. 30. D and F *omit*] and Young. l. 32. A and B] all uncivill, all such beasts as these. C] are uncivill, all such beasts. D and E] wee are uncivill, as such beasts as these. F and G] all uncivil. Would, etc.

p. 294, l. 7. G] are you. l. 11. A−C] learning new sir. E−G *omit*] Sir. l. 14. A] rouge. l. 16. A] capassions. l. 17. 2nd Folio *misprints*] Goaler. l. 25. F and G] indeed I do.

p. 295, l. 8. 2nd Folio *misprints*] A I. l. 27. F and G] Heaven quite. 1. 31. F and G] thou help. l. 34. F and G *omit*] the Cleve. l. 36. F] all this.

p. 296, l. 30. F, *some copies*] hankt it. l. 34. G] O Heaven.

p. 297, l. 1. F and G] with this. l. 12. F and G] who I. l. 17. B, F and G] hold out. l. 22. A] witnes to. ll. 26 and 27. F and G] this Welford from.

p. 298, l. 5. 2nd Folio *misprints*] turn. l. 8. A, B, D, F and G] tyr'd. l. 12. A] sore Ladies. D−G *omit*] four. l. 19. F and G] I think I. l. 23. A] I see by her. l. 38. A and E] make.

p. 299, l. 2. E−G] he is. l. 10. A and B] A will. C] I will. l. 13. F and G] make you well. l. 15. G] unconverted. l. 20. F and G] tell you. l. 26. B] yon. l. 34. F and G] Who's.

p. 300, l. 8. F and G] must wear. l. 9. G *omits*] Of. l. 19. A and B] pound. l. 22. E and F *omit*] a. l. 29. G] you wall graze. l. 30. F and G] once again. l. 33. F and G] your Worship. l. 38. G] Why now.

p. 301, l. 3. F and G] As fast as. l. 11. C] helps. l. 17. A and B *omit*] the. l. 24. F and G] and lead. l. 25. A−G *add*] Finis.

[During the passing of these sheets through the press, a copy of the quarto named G (1677, 'The Seventh Edition') has been found in England by the writer of this note. Its existence has been ignored by every previous editor of Beaumont and Fletcher, and, apparently, by English bibliographers, the folio of 1679 being presumed to be 'Ed. 7.' The knowledge that a copy existed in America led to a fruit-less search for it in English libraries, until accident, a few months ago, brought one to light in time to enable a collation of its text to be included in the above notes. It will be seen that many of the readings are of considerable interest.

A.R.W.]